TIME TWISTER

Ged Maybury

Hippo Books
Scholastic Publications Limited
London

Scholastic Publications Ltd.,
10 Earlham Street, London WC2H 9RX, UK

Scholastic Inc.,
730 Broadway, New York, NY 10003, USA

Scholastic Tab Publications Ltd.,
123 Newkirk Road, Richmond Hill,
Ontario L4C 3G5, Canada

Ashton Scholastic Pty. Ltd.,
PO Box 579, Gosford, New South Wales,
Australia

Ashton Scholastic Ltd.,
165 Marua Road, Panmure, Auckland 6,
New Zealand

First published in New Zealand by Ashton Scholastic
Limited, 1986

First published in the United Kingdom by Scholastic
Publications Limited 1987

Text copyright © Ged Maybury 1985
Cover designed by Kendal Baker

ISBN 0 590 7058 73

Made and printed by Cox & Wyman Ltd, Reading.

Chapter one

Forty-five minutes to go. Jason McArthur looked at his watch for the tenth time in less than a minute.

Boring, boring, boring, he thought. Idly he pressed the function stud of his watch. The display flicked from hours and minutes to seconds and tenths of seconds. 57, 58, 59, 00, 01 . . . He gazed in fascination at the dancing liquid crystal display. There goes my life, he thought, speeding away, second by second – wasting as we sit here doing nothing while the teacher waits for the stupid bell to ring. Jason wandered over to the window, leaned on the sill and continued his daydreaming. I hope old Mitch gives us back our games. He will. He's got to! He thought ahead to when they finally got out of school. I hope Dad remembered to ask if I could use the computer at the university during the holidays. I wonder how Mum is getting on? Maybe we'll get another letter today.

Next to Jason sat 'Muzz' Watson. This seating arrangement wasn't by choice – Muzz played up so much that Mr Mitchener had put him up the front with Jason.

"Hey, Sonny!" Muzz called to his friend and fellow troublemaker, over the rising hubbub of Room 13. "Hey!" He leaned across the aisle to poke Sonny in the ribs with his ruler.

Sonny twisted around with a loud grunt, revealing the fact that he and his deskmate were busy reading a comic below the edge of the desk.

"What've you got?" hissed Muzz.

"Nah! You've read it already. It's yours."

"Hey!" roared Muzz, "Gizza look, will ya?"

By now the whole class was rowdy and restless and Jason wasn't the only one out of his seat when 'Old Mitch' blew his whistle. Jason slunk quickly back to his desk and looked at the teacher expectantly.

"All right, Room thirteen . . . QUI-ET! We still have forty-five minutes of Term One to go, then you can make as much noise as you like for two whole weeks," Mr Mitchener shouted over the noise that had not quite died away, "*after* the bell at three o'clock! Now – " he pressed his advantage, "we still have a lot of tidying up to be done in that time. All the chairs and desks must be stacked in the centre of the room – when I say so, Ngahiwi! And you can be first on the broom."

"Aw, Sir!" moaned Sonny. Everyone was laughing at him. He had tried to balance his desk on the head of the boy behind him, but now his joke had backfired. He put the desk down, embarrassed.

"But first," continued Mr Mitchener, "I have to give you your homework." A huge grin spread

2

over his face as a wave of protest rose against him. He was joking, of course. "I'll tell you what. I'll postpone that homework till the first week of next term."

"Yay!" chorused the class. Now he had them.

"Actually, I want you all to write a short story during the first week of next term, entitled 'My Adventurous Holiday', so don't switch your brains off over the next two weeks – especially you, Murray Watson."

Muzz melted back to his seat and put on his 'Look-I'm-behaving-myself-now' face. The comic would have to wait.

"Thank you. As I was saying . . . don't switch off. I want you all thinking about that story. Remember everything that happens, places you go, people you meet . . . yes, Suzanne?"

"Can you make things up?"

"Well, I'd rather you reported your real life adventures. And if you don't think you had any adventures, then I still want you to write as though what you did was an adventure. Okay? Now, one last thing. I have two Space Invaders calculators that I confiscated during this term. Don't let me see these in class again. Got that, Watson? Pomare?"

"Yes, sir," chimed the boys in unison with unnaturally sweet voices. Mr Mitchener handed back the slim pocket computers with a meaningful scowl. The warning was quietly taken by at least half a dozen others in the room – the lucky ones who had evaded confiscation.

"Right! Let's get this room packed up."

Within seconds there was pandemonium, as desks were dragged and hoisted and crashed and stacked. Books, bags and brooms were moved to and fro in seeming confusion. Comics and conversations were enjoyed openly. Sounds like distant thunder boomed through the walls. Rooms 12 and 14 were at it too. Muzz took the opportunity amidst the confusion to slip the pocket computer back to Jason.

"Thanks for the loan," he said brightly.

"Yeah – thanks for returning it so quickly!" Jason replied sarcastically.

Restless minutes ticked away as a bright May afternoon beckoned to the prisoners of the unbending school bell timetable.

Finally, release. Bodies crushed through the doorway and burst out into the playground even before the bell had ceased ringing. Jason hung back. He kind of liked watching everyone scurrying off. It felt good to be different.

"Have a good holiday, Mr Mitchener," called Suzanne as she joined the moving throng.

"See ya, Mitch!" Muzz shouted from a safe distance, and took off.

Of course the boys headed straight for Moon Base. Only half a kilometre from the gates of the school, Bob Shakle's Seven-Days-a-Week shop did a roaring trade after school. Being a quick-witted businessman, Bob soon saw the potential in video games, and had hastily converted an over-sized storeroom into the 'Moon Base Video Parlour'. Total cost: half a day's carpentry, two litres of cheap paint, and the electrician's fee. It was definitely a big boost for business, and here they came again – the daily tide of school kids. Their boisterous energy frightened him a little, though he never let on about it. He knew perfectly well, however, that they all called him 'Old Shakey'.

Mouse arrived first. Only parents and teachers called him Brian – to everyone else he was plain 'Mouse'. What he lacked in size, however, he made up for in other ways. He did a spectacular rear-wheel skid in the car park by the butcher's, and flung his bike against the concrete back wall. His BMX could take that kind of treatment – just.

Moments later Tub, Sniff, Muzz and Sonny came flying into the car park, squealing their voices like a good sequence from 'The A Team'. Gravel and dust flew. Bikes clattered in a heap.

"Hey! Watch it!" yelled Tub. His bike somehow ended up on the bottom. No one paid any attention and they all jostled into the video games room.

"Hey, Sonny. Got any money?" Muzz, as usual, had none.

"Yeah, but . . ."

"Loan me twenty cents till tomorrow, will ya?"

"Mum gave me two dollars to buy the bread on my way home. I gotta keep the change or she'll kill me."

But Muzz had spotted silver. "What's that then?"

"That's mine. I kept it from my lunch money."

"Here – let me carry it for you," Muzz was all mock concern, "you must be exhausted after sweeping out the classroom."

"Nah! Got bigger muscles now, eh! Shove over, will ya, I wanna play."

Muzz persisted, "C'mon, Ngahiwi, just lend me twenty cents till after dinner. I'll be your friend for life. I'll pay ya back, promise."

Sonny was easy. Muzz always paid his debts.

"Oh . . . okay. Pay me back after dinner, all right?"

"Yeah, sure. Hey thanks, Sonny. You're cool!"

Meanwhile Mouse was going from game to game, religiously pressing the replay buttons. Sometimes – well, once – he'd scored a free game that way. Not today.

"Hey, Watson!" he called. "Your brain still switched on? Ha, ha, ha." Muzz swung a friendly kick at him. Mouse was too quick. One 'friendly' kick from Muzz Watson was enough. Sonny was quick, too. He bagged the Space Invaders machine. Space Invaders was old hat, and yet it still held a respected place at Moon Base. It was the measure against which all the other games were judged. The gang had had a long-standing battle for the top notch on this particular machine. It was like a friend which they fed often. Sonny fed it another twenty cents.

"Hey! Who's 'XXX'?" said Sniff. On the screen was the list of the ten best players. Each of them had a three-letter code. Sniff was 'SNF', Muzz was 'MUZ', and Sonny had chosen 'SOL' for some reason. Now a new codename was on the list. 'XXX'. Three times! Sniff swore. "He's shoved me right off the list, the bath-plug! He's better than Muzz too!"

"It's some guy from West High School," said Tub, matter-of-factly. In fact, he had no idea who it was.

"Ya reckon?" grunted Sniff in a way that let everyone know what he thought of Tub's opinion.

"Shut up, you guys!" Sonny was intent on his game, picking off electronic aliens as fast as he could. 'Boom!' He'd dodged right into an alien bomb. His audience laughed and jeered.

"Ah, c'mon Sonny . . ."

"Too much sweeping at school."

"Sweeping or sleeping?" That was Mouse.

"Shut up, you guys." Sonny just wasn't on form today, and the gang crowded around to watch him go down. Well before he'd run up a respectable score the aliens had won.

"Dammit. Hey, can I have my other twenty back? These jerks were putting me off."

Muzz was unsympathetic. He took over. "Nah. Now let me show you how an expert plays."

Mouse was in quickly, "Make way for Jase then, Muzz!"

Muzz shot him a hard little punch. Mouse was too quick for him, again. "Shut up Mouse," said Muzz as he shoved Sonny's coin into the slot, although secretly he acknowledged that Mouse did have a point. Jason McArthur was undoubtedly the expert when it came to playing Space Invaders, or any other game that came out for that matter. In fact Jason McArthur was the all-round whizz kid of the neighbourhood. Always top in maths and science. A real little know-all but at least he wasn't stuck-up like Joanne Mundy, and he did help Muzz out with his maths in class — a very important consideration, Muzz felt. So if anyone was okay with Muzz Watson, he was okay with the gang, but Jason *was* better at Space Invaders and that bugged Muzz. He thumped out his frustration on the controls. Alien invaders tumbled off the screen.

Actually, Jason was just outside, putting his bike in the bike stand. After dozens of complaints from little old ladies (so he'd heard) the Council had erected a bike stand, so the boys' gang had decided to park in the vacant lot instead. Besides, there was a lot of loose gravel there.

The girls' gang was also there for an end of term milkshake. His sister Helena was one of them. She called out, "Dad said be home early, Jase. Tell Troy."

"Yeah, okay. I'll wait for him." He turned from the bike stand and collided with Tracy Beatson, who had been shoved from behind.

"Give your boyfriend a kiss, Trace!" yelled Debbie Hammond, the chief pusher. Several other girls began chanting.

"Tracy and Jasie, Tracy and Jasie!"

8

Tracy had sprung away from the sudden contact. "Cut it out! We are not. Oh!" She went for Debbie, "Just because you can't . . ." Tracy scored a good swipe with her schoolbag, as Debbie's escape was foiled by the others pressing in behind.

"Can't what?" Debbie threw back. Tracy was satisfied with the one hit and said nothing. Debbie was going strange over boys. Helena was embarrassed. After all, it was her brother.

Jason slipped past them, pretending it hadn't happened. Within moments he was in the video games room. All the games were bleeping, buzzing, warbling and booming, like an undersea world of electronic whales and dolphins.

"Hey, here comes Jason." That was Tub — always inclined to state the obvious. Jason had a soft spot for Tub. He knew he was only trying to be liked and couldn't help being overweight.

"Yay! The champ!" Sniff proclaimed. "You're still top of the list, Jase."

"Uh-huh." Jason always tried hard not to seem too pleased with himself. But he was. It always surprised him how well he played these things. He was afraid that if he let himself become too proud about it, he'd lose the gift.

"How's your score, Sniff? Beaten it yet?"

"Nah. Not playing today. Broke. Besides, some bath-plug from West High has knocked me off the list. Triple X he calls himself. He's better than Muzz, even."

"I'll beat him," declared Muzz without looking up.

Jason studied the screen. Muzz was past 22,000. "What's he have to beat?"

"Thirty-five thousand. That's triple X's highest."

"Must be good. Hey Sonny! You got twenty cents?"

"Oh no! No, no, no!" Sonny would make a good actor. "Not again. No. I'm going crazy!" He rolled his eyes dramatically. "I'm off home or Mum'll kill me. See ya at school Monday, you guys!"

"Der! Ya dummy," said Sniff, talking like a moron. "It's the holidays, dummy. No – school – on – Monday. Got it?"

"Yeah, switch ya brain on, ha ha." Tub finally got a good dig in.

"Aw knock it off, all right. Hey Watson! Don't forget that twenty cents tonight."

"Okay. See ya, Sonny." replied Muzz. "Damn!" The game was over and Muzz had only scored 29,840. At least he could push XXX off tenth place.

Mouse was suddenly in the middle of the group. "Hey, you guys, there's a new game here. Old Shakey's put in a new game!"

"Hey! Good one!"

"What's it called?"

"Time Twister."

"You mean 'Time Pilots'. They aren't new," said Tub.

But Time Twister it was. In the far corner, opposite the door and stuck at a funny angle against the pinball machine, was the new game. It looked brand new and different somehow. The cabinet seemed to be moulded out of one piece of plastic, a metallic, warm, grey colour. It could have come straight out of a Star Wars movie or something.

The boys reverently stroked the moulded curves and hollows. It was warm to the touch and radiated a sense of power. Each one of them felt as they would upon opening a Christmas parcel to discover a very expensive present.

"Hey look! It's got a helmet." Sniff's eyes had moved to the top of the machine. Above the words 'Time Twister' which glowed as if lit from within, there was a strange upsweep in the cabinet and nestled within the curves, like a seed in a pod, was a helmet. He grasped it. It didn't budge.

Jason's eyes were quickly drawn to the screen and the controls. He found his hand naturally resting on the controls. They were well designed, with a place for the palm to rest so that the fingers were free to operate a bar-like switch. "Wow! Hey, that's amazing!" he exclaimed.

"What?"

"Look!"

The comfortable moulded handrests could actually slide up and down the front of the console at a slight angle perfectly suited to the natural swing of the arm. Yet there were no slots or any obvious mechanism that attached them to the machine.

"Magnets underneath," said Sniff, doubtfully.

"How d'ya play it, Jase?"

"Let's see. You take time jumps forwards or backwards. See, this is the time axis, up and down the screen. And these are what are called 'events' crossing the screen . . . oh, they go either way . . . "

Now the shifting patterns began to make sense. Blocks of colour, some pointed and some blunt, moved across the screen at various speeds. A bright, horizontal bar of light, about three centimetres long, rode upwards as the shifting pattern of events descended the screen. The bar of light had a word on it: NOW.

"Look! It's hit an event – it's being pulled off to one side – hey! It jumped! Everything's changed."

"No, it's the same pattern it was earlier."

"Jumped back? Negative five? What's that?"

"Time in the past. Five 'somethings'."

"It's caught again . . ."

"Pull it back to centre, now I'd jump."

"Another event, it's . . ."

"Jumped. Oh. Wrong timing. It's out." Each one of them had a dozen questions.

"How do you . . .?"

"Wait on! Look!"

★ ★ TIME TWISTER ★ ★

★ BY FUTURE PRODUCTS ★

★ ONE PLAYER ONLY ★

20c

USE LEFT OR RIGHT
HAND CONTROL

JUMP FORWARDS OR BACKWARDS IN TIME
TO AVOID CHANGING THE COURSE OF EVENTS

PENALTY POINTS FOR CHANGING THE COURSE
OF EVENTS AND FOR TIME SPENT
OFF COURSE

BONUS TIME UNITS FOR EACH RETURN TO 'NOW'
WHILE ON CENTRE LINE

BONUS POINTS FOR RIDING GREEN EVENTS
PENALTY POINTS FOR RIDING RED EVENTS

TIME JUMP RESERVE: 80 UNITS

Muzz had joined them unnoticed. Suddenly he spotted something. "Hey! It's got a helmet!" He grabbed it. "Aw, it doesn't come off."

"Probably does when you put your money in."

"Yeah, I bet it comes off when you put your money in."

"Yeah – like your head, Tub," said Mouse. "Okay, who's gonna play? Go on, Jase, you're the ace. Give it a go!"

"Anyone got a twenty?" asked Jason.

"Nope, I spent mine." Muzz sounded disappointed.

"Wasn't yours, it was Sonny's," Tub corrected him.

"So what! Big deal, Tub!" Muzz flung back.

Tub had the knack of getting up everyone's nose sooner or later. He was saved this time by the arrival of Jason's older brother, Troy.

"Hey, Troy! Troy! Come and have a look at this! They've got a new machine. Hey! You got twenty cents?"

"Sorry, baby brother — I'm flat broke till tonight. Tough!" Troy was only a third former at West High, but here, among Jason's mates, he was acting big. "Hey! What *is* this thing?"

Several explanations began at once. Troy got the drift of it before long and became interested. "I might have some jingle in my pencil-case." He rummaged around in his bag. "Hang on . . . ten cents, a two, another two, a five — and another two. Twenty-one cents."

"I'll change it." Mouse took the coins and sped off to the shop counter.

Behind him he heard Troy say "Hey, it's got a helmet . . ."

Bob Shakle was at the counter. "Another game of pinball, eh?" he said, handing Mouse the twenty cent piece.

"No, we're playing Time Twister. The new game."

"What new game?"

"You know, Time Twister. You've just got it. Thanks." The boy grabbed the coin and was off. Bob stood puzzled. He shrugged, "Kids!"

"Gee Old Shakey's slow," reported Mouse. "He doesn't even know he's got a new game!"

"Well," announced Troy. "My money, my game."

The coin slipped smoothly into the slot. A

snatch of electronic music played, and the helmet lit up.

"Wow!"

The helmet came freely into Troy's hands. There didn't seem to be anything keeping it there at all. A spiral cord, like a telephone cord, still joined it to the top of the cabinet. Troy looked inside it carefully. The inside was made of the same stuff as the outside. He felt it. It was quite soft. Satisfied, he put it on. Everyone was silent. Troy placed his hand on the control and the game began.

"Hey, what's the helmet like on?" asked Sniff.

"Shhh!" said someone else.

Troy hardly heard them. From the moment he had put the helmet on, everything seemed distant and unreal, except himself and the Time Twister. He felt very alert and strangely powerful. Intently he watched the screen. Jason had been pushed aside by the jostling crowd and could barely see the screen, so he watched Troy instead.

"Look out!"

"Jump!"

"Jump back!"

The boys all yelled their advice. Troy eased the control down a bit and touched the switch. The patterns on the screen changed completely. He had dodged one danger and now faced another. Already he was off course. If he could just jump forward a tiny bit he could ride that green event back to the central course. In his intense concentration he hardly noticed that he was alone. The other boys simply were not there. It was very quiet all about him. He took a tiny jump and caught the green event. In the back of his mind he wondered where the others had gone but he didn't have time to look around for them because he had reached the central line. He jumped back to 'Now'.

Suddenly the boys were back around him, shouting noisily. Jason had been watching Troy. For an instant he had seemed to flicker, like a bit missing from a film. Troy suddenly seemed startled and tense. He played on.

"Jump forward!" someone yelled.

Almost angrily, Troy pushed up the control grip and his fingers stabbed the switch. An instant passed, and in that instant, Troy had changed. Changed a lot. Jason had noticed but no one else had, they were all too intent on the game. But Jason had seen his brother transformed in that instant. Now Troy was heaving for breath, a wild and frightening look in his eyes. His school uniform was crumpled and dirty with a few bits of twig and dead leaves caught on it. In that instant a gasp escaped between those ragged breaths. He spun away from the machine, his wild eyes settled on Jason and held him hard.

Chapter two

As Troy left the Time Twister controls, the others protested.

"Hey, don't . . . "

"You can't just . . . "

"I'll take over," Muzz jumped in instantly. "It's . . . "

"Saved it!"

"Why'd ya stop, Troy?"

"You play, I . . . " Troy didn't finish. He seemed lost for words.

"You all right?" asked Jason, anxiously.

"Yep. Okay now." Troy's breathing had eased.

Behind them the game went on. The others clamoured to shout advice and warnings. Troy leaned on the pinball machine, filled with so much to say, yet said nothing. He gazed into space, holding his breath, until Jason had to say something.

"Dad said be home early."

"Dad!" Troy spun around, his face a mixture of emotions. "Is he all right?"

"Course he is!" said Jason, although he suddenly felt doubtful, and resisted a sudden wave of fear from the pit of his stomach that threatened to engulf him. What did Troy know that he didn't? "He should be home by now," he stated with false conviction.

The game had finished. Muzz had played well, or so the gang thought.

"Fifteen hundred points. Not bad."

Sniff was fascinated with the helmet. "Gizza look, will ya, Troy?" he asked. Troy absently passed it over, then strode out. Sniff tried it on.

"What's it like?" asked Mouse.

"Nothing. Doesn't do anything."

"Just a fake."

"Yeah, I bet it's a fake," agreed Tub.

"I'd better put it back."

"Gimme a look first," protested Mouse.

Too late. The helmet seemed to jerk out of Sniff's hands as he went to replace it. With a buzzing clunk it locked itself back into place.

"Hey, Troy! What about your bag?" His school bag still sat on the pinball machine. Jason took the bag and ran after Troy. It was only seconds before Jason reached the street but already Troy was a small figure in the distance, running for home.

Jason's sense of alarm soon faded. In the late afternoon sunlight everything seemed normal. It was autumn, and the crisp, still air was filled with the smell of damp, fallen leaves. The trees were still dressed in golden rags. He picked up his bike and followed, enjoying his race after Troy through the magical afternoon, and soon the events at Moon Base were blown away by the rush of cold air down those reassuringly familiar streets.

Helena was home. She and a friend were practising gymnastics on the front lawn. Troy pounded up breathlessly.

"Is Dad home?"

"Yeah. He's in the shower. Boy, are you a mess! Been fighting again?"

"No. No, I . . . oh nothing, just . . . some of those big jerks on the bus. Is Dad all right?"

"Of course! Why, what's the matter?"

"Oh nothing. I – I just had a funny dream about him, that's all."

"Uh-huh. Hold my legs, will you?" Helena turned to her friend and went into a handstand.

Jason had put his bike away. He had pretty well convinced himself by now that Troy had been playing a game. They met in the kitchen.

"I'm going to change," said Troy, still breathing hard. "Don't go away, will ya."

"Okay. Wanna drink?" Jason called from behind the fridge door. Troy didn't reply. He wasn't there.

Jason was pouring an orange juice when his father came in, still towelling his hair. "Hi, Jase. Glad it's all over?"

"What? Oh, school. Yeah. Wanna juice?"

"Yes please. Thanks." Dave McArthur sipped his juice. But he was savouring something else – he had some good news for Jason. "Guess what?"

"What?" Jason looked blank.

"It's all arranged. You've got half an hour on the big one every day for the next two weeks."

19

"Wow! Really? Far out! Thanks, Dad." Jason was thrilled. He had been waiting for this for weeks, ever since his father had suggested that Jason have a go on the new Programming Research Computer, recently installed in Dave's department at the university.

"But you've got to be there at eight-thirty in the morning."

"Eight-thirty! Oh shi – shivers. That's earlier than school!"

"What a shame," said Dave sarcastically. "No sleeping in all holidays. Anyway, it'll keep you busy. Ha! You'll beat that big ol' computer yet, knowing you. Now, what's for tea?"

"Dunno," shrugged Jason with exaggerated casualness, "you're the cook."

"Dad!" Troy came bursting in between them and wrapped his father in an uncharacteristic embrace.

"Crikey, Troy." Dave was taken aback. "I've only been away since this morning. What's up? I mean, thanks for the hug, but . . . "

"Well, I'm just glad to see you . . . home. That's all." Troy was suddenly embarrassed.

"Didn't you say you had a bad dream about Dad last night?" Jason asked helpfully.

"Yeah, that's it. That's why . . . hey, what's for dinner, Dad? Can we have pizza tonight? Huh?"

Dave readily agreed. Pizza was his forte. Besides, the whole conversation needed a change of direction. "Now buzz off and give me some cooking room – unless of course you want to do this morning's dishes . . . ?"

"I've got some homework," said Troy.

"Me too," added Jason. "Sort of – anyway, there'll be more after dinner, so we may as well do them all then." He took off after Troy.

Dave stood for a while, amused. But behind his smile he wondered about his eldest son. What was up with Troy?

Dinner was uneventful. The pizza was first class as always. 'Just like a bought one,' as Dave often said. Troy, Jason and Helena always disagreed. 'It's better!' they would say.

They shared a lot of small talk about this and that, and plenty of joking around, but each one of them missed Natty, though no one said so. Natisha McArthur was in Tonga, teaching English under the Volunteer Service Abroad scheme. It was something she'd always wanted to do, so now that her children were older and Dave was established in his new appointment with time enough to cope with the changes, she had gone. She wrote often and it all sounded like a great adventure, though she had her ups and downs. Another letter was due any day.

"Well, boys," Dave leaned back at last. "Dishes."

Troy and Jason did some fast talking and managed to forestall the inevitable. Once in their bedroom, Jason shut the bedroom door behind them. "Now," he said. "Tell all, O Weird One!"

21

"Okay. As promised, here goes." Before dinner he'd promised to tell Jason the reason for his strange behaviour after playing the Time Twister. "Swear you won't tell anyone?" he demanded for about the fifth time.

"Yeah, yeah. Okay. Just get on with it."

Troy paused, assembling his thoughts with difficulty. "You won't believe this. I'm not sure I do either." He drew a deep breath and began.

★ ★ ★

Troy hit the button. His life changed. It was dark. All was silent. Beneath his hands was the Time Twister. The screen was on but showed no pattern or movement. Fear and confusion struck him. He spun around. No one. No one! Where? How? Why? His heart was trying to leap out of his chest. It was Moon Base. Still the same old place, but dark. Power failure? Yes. No! It was daytime, wasn't it? He hurried to the front door. Locked! Night-time outside the glass. A deserted street. Troy's mind went blank. He shivered.

Home. Must get home! There was a back door for deliveries. Stealthily he let himself out. It clicked shut behind him, loudly. He ran. It was cold. It had just been raining. How? Why? He wanted to cry, but held back the tears.

"Hey, you!" A shout rang out, halting him in his tracks. He stopped, poised like a wild animal, panting. Across the road were two men. Soldiers?

Uniforms, dark green, like bottles. Straps. Belts. Weapons. Radios. Caps. Walking towards him. Run! screamed his mind.

"What are you doing out?" demanded the closest man.

Troy ran through the church grounds towards the creek.

"Stop!"

He didn't. The air around him buzzed strangely and blew warm for a moment on his face. Around the corner, through the hedge, past the church hall. He dived between fence and shrubs, down and a twist, a familiar action. Now he felt safe, in home territory.

For several kilometres the creek meandered through low ground behind many subdivisions. A child's world of tree-huts, bush caves, secret ways, water, mud, rope swings, bike tracks. In the dark, Troy silently melted away, following paths that only children use. He heard no sounds of pursuit. Home! Must get home! Across the pipe. Under the bridge. To the back fence. The house was lit up — much too lit up. Every light seemed to be on. Why? What now? He slipped through the garage then froze.

Soldiers. Everywhere. The same dark green. He watched from the shadows. No, only five of them really. In the street two vehicles stood waiting. Dark machines, big and dangerous, like tanks. On their sides was painted a sign or symbol. A planet within the letter C. Why do they wait? Why here?

Suddenly, out of the front door marched more soldiers. In their midst was another person. "Dad!" With a scream, Troy burst from cover. "Leave him alone!" he shouted, hitting wildly at green uniforms. A whirling mass of figures surrounded him, hands grabbing. He dodged, leaping a flower bed.

"Troy! Run!" He and his father jumped the low front fence and sprinted down the footpath. Shouts followed them, orders. The air buzzed and hummed. The sound jangled on his nerves. His father pitched forwards on the grass, stiff, twitching. "Run, Troy!" he croaked. The air buzzed again, hot and electric. A searchlight swung through the tree-tops. Troy swallowed a sob and ran. Through a front yard, down a driveway, towards the creek. Away. Away to hide. Away to cry.

★ ★ ★

"I hid in the bush cave all night. Those guys searched a few times with torches. They must have given up after a bit. I stayed awake. Seemed like ages. I didn't know what time it was. My watch still said it was today. By the time it got light it still only said a quarter past nine. Look." Troy showed Jason his watch.

It read 12.24 a.m. He pressed a stud. Saturday's date. Jason's mind sought a rational explanation. He must have changed it himself, he thought.

"I haven't touched it," said Troy, as if he had read Jason's thoughts. "It's proof. Proof that . . . "

He didn't finish. Troy was finding it just as hard to believe as Jason was.

"Anyway, I got back. Boy, was that a relief! I was so freaked out about Dad." His voice began to shake and he drew a deep breath. He hadn't let on just how much he'd cried back there. "Getting back was . . . " Once again tears threatened to escape.

"How?"

"Huh?"

"How'd ya get back?" Jason was as keen to change the subject as Troy was. Troy's tears were more proof than the watch and that frightened Jason. Troy continued his unbelievable account.

★ ★ ★

Stiff and sore he wormed out of the low, dry hollow beneath the bushes. With eyes and ears on full alert he retraced his course. Green uniforms in the street. Vehicles. That insignia again. His home was surrounded. He crept away without hope, convinced that World War Three had begun.

★ ★ ★

"I was really hungry so I went down the creek to the Manor Road bridge and then down the lane to Shakey's. I'd remembered that I'd left my school bag there and figured on cashing in my bus concession ticket for something. People were looking at me real funny. Just staring. That was because

I still had the helmet on I suppose. Ha! Crazy, eh, I'd had it on all that time and didn't even realize it! So there I was, standing in the doorway of Shakey's, trying to get up the guts to go in, when around the corner came two of those guards or whatever they were.

"I ducked inside but they'd seen me. I guess I just sort of panicked then. I ran to the Time Twister, which was the only machine going in the whole place and just stood there, like a dummy. It was only then that I realized that I still had the helmet on, and something finally clicked in my head. 'Time Twister'! It actually worked. I was – somewhere else in time."

Troy looked straight at Jason. "I was nearly too late. The soldiers were coming, so I grabbed it and yelled 'Go' or something. I was really scared and knew it just *had* to work. Then – Bam! All the guys were yelling 'Jump, jump'. You were there and . . . well, you know the rest."

Jason was silent. Could it be true? "You're pulling my leg, aren't you? C'mon . . ."

"No, I'm not, dammit!" Troy shouted. "Here!" he picked up his shoe and sock. "Look!"

Jason examined the evidence before him. The shoe was muddy and damp with traces of fine gravel inside. The sock was also damp and smelled of creek mud.

"I stood in the creek last night. Last night, whenever I'd time-jumped to." He saw the doubt on Jason's face. "Look – was I anywhere near the creek this afternoon?"

Jason's mind whirled with the implications. He didn't answer.

"Troy! Jason! What about these dishes?" called their father, thumping on their bedroom door as he passed. Both boys jumped with fright.

"Okay, coming."

Jason almost leapt from the room, relieved to escape from their weird conversation. Dishes he understood. Dishes were something real and normal. He had never before wanted to do the dishes as much as he wanted to right now. Troy felt much the same.

"I'll wash!" shouted Jason.

"I'll wash – aw." Troy was too slow. "Okay, I'll dry."

Dave settled himself at the kitchen table with a sigh. From his briefcase he pulled out folders, reports, textbooks, unmarked exam papers and an assortment of things collected during the term. Finally he pulled out a slim document in a dark green folder.

"How on earth did this get in here?" he muttered to himself. The cover was plain except for one thing – a circular symbol. A globe or planet within the letter C.

"Hey! We're out of detergent," announced Jason.

"Yay!" cheered Troy as he hung up his tea towel with exaggerated flair.

"Do them without," suggested Dave.

"They're too greasy, Dad."

"Okay – you'd better run down and get some then. I think we need some more milk anyway." Dave began digging in his pocket for money.

"Yep. None left," confirmed Troy, slamming the fridge door.

"Well, who's going? Shackle's should still be open."

"Ah . . ." Troy hesitated. Shackle's meant Moon Base.

"I'll go," said Jason quickly, sensing his brother's fear.

"Righto. Here's two dollars. No, you might need more." Dave pulled out a handful of change and dumped it into Jason's open palm. Jason was halfway down the path when he remembered the milk bottles. He rushed back inside and grabbed the crate, grinning sheepishly, before slamming the door behind him.

In the silence that followed Troy wandered over to where Dave was shuffling through his papers. "What'ya doing, Dad?"

"My homework. Done yours?" he asked.

"Got none!" Troy replied smugly. He glanced down at his father's 'homework', and saw something that made his blood run cold. It was as if a doorway to another world had opened. A nightmare world of running, soldiers, shouts, his father falling, twitching . . . Troy opened his eyes wide. There sat his father just across the table, safe and unhurt. Troy eased his trembling body onto a chair. He gathered himself together enough to ask casually, "Dad, what was your day like?"

"Absolutely hectic." Dave didn't look up. "Typical end of term. Look at me — still trying to catch up."

If that was a hint, Troy didn't get it. He wanted to know something. Trying to exhibit only idle curiosity, he took the slim, green folder and waved it slightly. "What's this?"

"Huh? Oh, that. Nothing too exciting, I'm afraid. Actually it shouldn't even be here. It's confidential. It seems to have got itself into my briefcase instead of several other things." Dave ceased rummaging through his papers and tossed them aside with a frustrated sigh. He took the folder from Troy.

"It's a proposal from Computer Link Overlock, 'COMPLOK' for short. It's a new technical services company in the computer world, they specialize in computer link security. Anyway, they are negotiating with my department to establish a temporary working link with our new Program Research Computer. It's all politics, really. This is just technical stuff." He tossed it onto the pile of papers. "I'm supposed to approve the whole thing by Tuesday," he admitted unenthusiastically.

"Don't!" burst out Troy.

"What?"

Troy was silent. The word had leapt out of his mouth before he could stop it. Now he struggled for some sort of explanation.

"Don't what, Troy? What's up, son?"

Troy sat in silence.

"Come here, Troy-boy. We obviously need more time together. All of us."

Troy hadn't been called Troy-boy for years and at any other time he would have felt most offended. But at this point it was just what he needed. Gratefully he surrendered to his father's warm embrace.

Jason parked his bike and went inside the shop. His hands and face tingled from the cold evening air. The shop was ablaze with lights but completely deserted. He tucked his hands under his armpits and surveyed the shelves.

"Detergent, detergent . . . ah, here it is. Dad always gets the yellow one." He put the detergent bottle on the counter along with the two empty milk bottles in their crate.

"In the cooler. Help yourself," called Bob Shackle from the back of the shop. Jason searched in the cooler for bottles of milk.

"Can't find any."

"Bottom shelf." Bob came out from behind the counter.

"None there. Just cream."

"Hang on, I'll get another crate," said Bob and disappeared out the back of the shop.

From beside the cooler Jason could see into the video games parlour. Every game was off and the lights too, except for a soft greenish glow. Curious, Jason drifted through the doorway.

It was the Time Twister. In the quiet room he

became aware of the faint sound of music in the air. The Time Twister seemed to draw him towards it. There was something about this thing that he had to investigate. Compelled by some instinct he reached into his pocket for a twenty cent coin and stepped in front of the screen.

Chapter three

Helena sensed something was wrong with Troy. She also knew that sooner or later she would find out, so it came as no surprise when her father stuck his head through the door and said, "Helena, come and have a cup of cocoa with us in the kitchen."

"Just a minute. I want to watch this first."

Dave didn't argue. It was an item about modern dance. Helena stayed glued to the television until the programme finished. She came pirouetting into the kitchen, narrowly missing an open cupboard door with her whirling limbs, and ended in a back-stretching, splayfooted pose on the kitchen table.

"So what's up?" she asked.

"Your left arm," retorted Dave quickly.

"Ha, ha, ha," said Helena, lazily lowering the gracefully poised arm and unbending her body.

"You know what I mean. What's cooking?"

"Nothing," said Dave, innocently glancing at the oven.

"Aaargh!" she exclaimed in frustration. She knew she wouldn't get any information out of her father until he was good and ready. She had noticed, however, that Troy was intently watching the kettle with his face turned away from her. She guessed he had been crying.

"Where's Jase?" she said.

It was more than curiosity, it was a compulsion. Jason *had* to play this game, wear the helmet, touch the live controls. Deep inside he felt an echo of a memory that he had known this thing before. Or was it the other way round?

"Games are all off. I'm closing up now. Here's your milk." The storekeeper's voice burst into Jason's dreamlike state.

"Okay." He retreated from the Time Twister which immediately seemed to dim. "Tomorrow, maybe."

Soon he was pedalling like mad to get back to the warm kitchen before his fingers froze. The nights were certainly growing colder.

"Ah, here's the milk," said Dave as Jason walked in the door.

He ceremoniously added milk to the four steaming mugs on the bench and passed them around. Jason gratefully wrapped his cold fingers around the hot mug as he huddled at the table, still puffing from his energetic ride.

"And now it's family announcement time," began Dave. "Due to a recent lack of caring and sharing in the McArthur household, it has been decided, now that school holidays are here, that members of the McArthur family will spend more time with each other and be attendant to each other's needs." He paused and looked at each of them in turn with a guilty expression. "Beginning with me."

They all gave him an encouraging smile, happy to see him acting more like his old self again. It had become a bit chaotic lately. Their father had been working overtime to ensure they got off to school on time, to do the washing, housework, cooking and shopping – all the things that Natty used to do that they never even noticed. They had all pitched in, of course, and did very well. But some special ingredient had sometimes gone missing. Tempers had flared some mornings and many evenings had passed in uncomfortable silence.

"We all miss Natty. I'm sure she misses us. We'd hoped initially that she would be able to come back for a quick holiday about now, but as you know that's proved impossible, so we'll all have to squeeze up and make up for the love that's missing," and he wrapped all three of them together with his long arms.

They all felt a little embarrassed to be so close together, but they each had a lump in their throat, too.

"So we'll start by all going camping this weekend!"

"Yay!" chorused Troy, Jason and Helena. The embarrassing moment had passed. At once they began discussing, planning, debating. After another round of cocoa, and French toast as well this time, it was decided they would head for 'McArthur's Park'.

Three hours drive from the city and they were in another world. The road twisted and turned up long, bush-choked valleys and crossed fresh, cold, mountain rivers. Rugged, dark green mountains crowded the horizon, some with bald heads of hard, grey rock and great, bright patches of last year's snow. It was actually called Arthur's Pass National Park. But for many years the McArthur family had come camping here, and Helena at four years old had named their favourite camp site 'McArthur's Park' after a song she'd heard on the radio one day. The name stuck.

It was different this time. It was autumn and the days were short and cold. Natty was in Tonga. But the drive up was beautiful; the landscape was full of red and gold trees, and long shadows hid pools of frost from the low, hazy sun. Besides, camping was always fun. Pitching tents, gathering firewood, making beds in the back of the station wagon, fetching water and eating smoke-flavoured food.

That night the McArthur family built a huge camp fire and sat on the dividing line between being roasted and being frozen. Sparks rushed furiously towards the cold, bright stars, dying on the way. The sky was breathtaking, the silence deep. The fire was the centre of their world. Marshmallows sizzled and drooped on the ends of skilfully twisting sticks, and a moment's laughter challenged the eternal cool peace of the beech forest.

Sitting there, both Jason and Troy mulled over

memories of the previous day. Was it only yesterday? Already it seemed far away and unreal, like a dream. They hadn't spoken of the Time Twister since that conversation in their room. It was all too much to handle really, too strange to talk about again so soon. After a night's sleep followed by a busy day, their minds had worked the story over, editing out the unacceptable and changing a few of the facts here and there.

Yes, Troy decided. It must have been a dream. I must have suddenly remembered it all in a rush at Moon Base. A dream . . . yes, that makes sense. He tried to erase it from his mind completely by thinking of the holidays ahead. His classmates were going to go roller-skating every day if they were allowed. Although it was a long bike ride, Troy intended to join them.

Another night's sleep should have finished the matter off but that night, as they tossed and turned, Troy had a nightmare. His classmates had turned into green uniformed guards and chased him down an endless video arcade. The games buzzed at him and flung out shots of burning fire. On one screen he could see his father who kept falling and falling. He woke in panic and lay for a long time listening to the comforting sound of Jason's steady breathing.

Jason had dreamed too, one of those crazy dreams like something out of a science fiction movie, but by morning he could not remember any of it. Nevertheless he was left with the impression that it was about something really important.

It was a perfect day and they took a long hike up the Three-Mile Creek track to the waterfall where they had lunch. Beneath the endless green roof of the beech forest, shafts of sunlight beamed down to spotlight the mossy glades, and a quiet peacefulness finally settled on the McArthur family. Eventually, in silence, they hiked back to camp. Helena had developed a bad blister but didn't mention it for fear of spoiling the atmosphere. Instead, she limped on in brave silence.

The sun slowly dropped in the sky as they packed the car, and cold, damp air had begun to seep out from the trees by the time they were ready to go.

"Sorry, kids," said Dave. "I wish I didn't have to attend that blasted meeting tomorrow." He sighed deeply. Dave loved this place as much as the children did. Nobody said anything more but breathed a final breath of fresh mountain air before getting in the car.

They stopped at Shackle's on the way home to get something quick and easy for tea. Jason recognized the heap of bikes on the footpath outside and went to meet the gang while Dave roamed the shop's shelves.

The gang were playing Time Twister. Their gestures of casual familiarity as they stood around the machine made the thing seem harmless and unmagical – just another video game. He noticed that although someone was busy playing a game, the helmet remained in its place. Tub wasn't there, but Sniff, Sonny and Mouse were — and Muzz Watson, of course, acting the big shot as always. Jason soon found out why.

"Hey! Where the hell've you been all weekend?" he called to Jason. "Been hiding, eh?" He went on to suggest several activities that Jason might have been up to. Jason told him very matter-of-factly that he'd been camping.

"Where?"

"Arthur's Pass."

"Freeze yer butt off?" Muzz asked, obviously showing off. Jason had no time to reply, because at that moment the unfamiliar boy who had been playing on the machine let loose a flood of bad language and kicked the Time Twister two or three times.

"Oi, knock it off, Steve! You're not in Greyport now!" Muzz joked. "Hey, this is Jase McArthur, I was telling you about. Jase, this is my cousin, Steve, from the Coast."

"Hi."

"Gidday," replied Steve, so closely scrutinizing Jason that he began to wonder just what Muzz had been saying about him. "Have a go," offered Steve, nodding at the new video game.

"Who's champ?" Jason asked, fumbling in his pockets for the correct coin.

"Me!" Muzz exclaimed boastfully. "And you'll never catch up now!"

Jason reached for the helmet. "It's fake," Sniff informed him.

"Yeah, just a gimmick," added Sonny.

"Oh?" Jason hesitated. "How do you know?"

"Coz I said so," proclaimed Muzz proudly. "I tried it out on Friday and it didn't do nothing, so there's no point in wearing it, is there?"

Jason shrugged. It didn't surprise him at all, the world was full of gimmicks. He pushed his coin into the slot.

"Jason!" It was his father. "We're going!"

Jason hesitated. Twenty cents was twenty cents.

"All right, you can run home. Dinner will be in about half an hour, okay?"

"Okay, thanks Dad."

Jason turned to the Time Twister and played his first game. Then another. He was beginning to get the hang of it. Muzz had a game. Sniff and Sonny began to fret about the time and being late for dinner, but stayed for one more game, hoping to see Muzz go down. Eventually they managed to drag themselves away. "Mum'll kill me," said Sonny as he finally walked through the door. Mouse went too. Steve played another game, then Muzz Watson's father came marching in, fuming.

"Murray! Didn't I tell you to be home by six? Your mother's worried sick! Don't you ever think about anyone but yourself? Now, come on." Muzz sloped away quietly with his father, and Steve tagged along behind grinning secretly to Jason.

Within moments the place had become deserted, but Jason didn't mind. All that movement and chatter had been distracting, and this new game was really intriguing him now. He simply had to play it again because it was different, and therefore challenging. A good player relied heavily on memory and sense of dimension.

Not unnaturally Jason liked to find things out for himself, so now that the others had all gone, he felt he could do his own test on the fake helmet without seeming an idiot. He put it on. It was lightweight and comfortable and seemed to fit perfectly.

He took it off and then put it on again, listening for any change and closely watching the screen as well. Nothing happened. He shrugged but left it on all the same. Another thing he had been wondering about was if the pattern of events that rolled down the screen ever repeated itself at some period in the time sequence. Jason decided to find out. Pushing the play button, he pulled down on the hand piece and touched the jump control.

★　★　★

There was an explosion of light and heat and sound. He jerked backwards instinctively and his feet seemed to go through the floor. He dropped panic-stricken through space, but only for a moment, then his feet struck a springy, uneven surface and he fell onto his backside. There he sat, completely dumbfounded. In front of him was a large, fallen tree, and slightly beyond that was the Time Twister. It was there, but it wasn't there; poised in mid-air and semi-transparent. It reminded Jason of a holographic image he had once seen at a science display. Through this image and all around him Jason could see tall trees of many different species. They were waving and tossing in a wild, hot wind and the sun beat down from high in a brilliant blue sky.

Jason sat awhile, slowly taking it all in and relaxing in the warmth. His heartbeat slowed to normal and he no longer felt afraid. The whole place felt incredibly familiar, and he now realized what had happened.

"Time travel," he whispered to himself. "Time travel."

He was somewhere in the past, sitting in the native bush prior to settlement in these parts. He looked at his surroundings with renewed interest. Three of the tree types he could name without any trouble: rimu, totara and kahikatea. He had never seen such magnificent trees before. "How absolutely amazing!" he said out loud, and in that distant day Jason McArthur laughed and laughed in the crazy, hot, northwest wind.

Time travel! The whole idea was incredibly exciting and his head spun at the thought of it. He touched his head and was reassured to find that the helmet was still firmly in place. It was so light that it was easy to forget he had it on. All was safe. He could return at any time.

Jason stood and moved closer to the Time Twister. As he approached it seemed to become more solid and real, and he figured that the helmet must have had something to do with that. He took it off and the video machine vanished in an instant. Quickly he replaced the helmet. This was one hat he must never lose!

Being such a nice day, Jason decided to explore a little. Carefully, he studied the place where he had landed, noting several good landmarks: a pair of tall, branching trees and another close by, growing out at a peculiar angle. He also hung his jacket on a head-high, jutting branch. The bright colours would stand out from a considerable distance.

Jason headed off, stopping frequently to get his bearings. The forest was magnificent and breathtakingly beautiful. Ahead of him the bush seemed to end and soon he could see the familiar outline of the Port Hills although they were covered in native bush and the television and radio masts were not there. A little further on he found an area where the bush had been felled. Logs and piles of cut scrub and branches littered the uneven ground. Further off, a few trees still stood, swaying unhappily, exposed to the full force of the wind. Several rough shacks had been built in the clearing. Jason was shocked and stunned by the scene of destruction before him.

Suddenly a loud noise made him jump. The sounds of axes ringing out on live wood were only a few metres to his right. He shrank back out of sight as he saw three men coming from the same direction, picking their way along the shattered edge of the forest. They carried axes and a long, curving saw with a handle on each end. They were dressed in heavy boots, dark, uncomfortable-looking trousers with braces, and collarless, white shirts.

"Blimmin' 'ot, innit?" called one of the men. Jason froze. The man seemed to be looking straight at him. Had he been seen? Should he reply? The chopping sound away to the right stopped.

"Aye, too bleedin' hot for a cuppa tea!" boomed a voice.

"Aye," replied the first man. "Sure an' if you ask Mrs Winthrop nice enough she'll fetch ye out a barrel o' Tanner's next time!"

"And pigs'll fly!" snorted the hidden axeman. They all laughed and resumed their work.

Jason was intrigued with their curious, old-fashioned accents and was torn between staying in the hope of hearing more, and the urge to sneak away unseen and get home as quickly as possible. An awful thought sent a shiver up his spine. What if he became trapped in this time? He'd never see his family again. And how would it affect them – his sudden disappearance?

Jason crept back deeper into the trees until he felt safe enough to move quickly and openly. Somehow, in his rush, he missed his track and had to force his way through some very thick patches of undergrowth. He couldn't see his landmarks anywhere. Feeling that he had perhaps veered too far to the left, he turned a fraction to his right and pressed on. He was lost, and his heart thumped in panic. He stopped. Above the roaring of the wind he could still faintly hear the axemen working behind him.

A few steps further on Jason came to a wet, swampy patch of ground and stopped again. Although he hadn't seen it before, the swamp was reassuring as it meant he had gone too far. He turned around and immediately spotted his brightly coloured windcheater through the tree trunks off to his left. With a sigh of relief he headed straight towards it, approaching from almost the opposite direction than the one in which he had left only half an hour before.

As he entered the slight clearing, the Time Twister image sprang into being again. To Jason this was further proof that it was projected by the helmet which he touched again in a gesture of reassurance. He pulled on his jacket and paused to place a couple of pine cones in his pocket. Then he wasted no further time. This beautiful place suddenly seemed threatening.

He leapt up on to the big log.

"Home, home," he murmured. He concentrated but nothing happened. His throat all at once felt dry, and he struggled to remain calm, to quell the fear rising inside him. He thought back to Troy's experience – Troy was being chased and was desperate, and he had just grabbed at the Time Twister. It wasn't much to go on. Jason reached out to the control and although he couldn't actually feel it, he could move it. Good. Then he imagined he was playing the game at Moon Base, and pushed the control forward, up towards his time – towards NOW. Panic welled up inside him.

"Now!" he shouted aloud, and jabbed the button.

★   ★   ★

Jason stumbled up the back steps and quietly came in the door. He felt exhausted. The wind, sun, fighting the undergrowth and nervous tension had completely drained him. On top of the long walk with his family that morning, the short walk home from the dairy had seemed the longest one of all.

The table had just been set. "That was good timing!" said Dave, turning from the stove with a steaming pot. The kitchen was warm and bright and full of the smells of toast and cheese and baked beans.

"It's good to be home!" stated Jason with more feeling than he had intended.

"Hear, hear," Dave agreed. "Sour cream, anybody?"

Chapter four

Jason was in a deep sleep when a gentle hand shook him awake.

"Come on, son, it's nearly eight o'clock." A pair of sleepy eyes looked blankly up at Dave McArthur. "The computer. Do you still want a go at it? Eight-thirty to nine was the only time I could get you."

"Oh, yeah, of course. Give me a minute, though."

"Sit up first." Slowly Jason sat up and swung his feet to the floor. He felt stiff and sore from the previous day although all he could remember was walking endlessly through native forests.

"Okay," said his father, "I'll make you some toast while you get dressed. It's cold out. You can come with me in the car."

Jason sat silently in the car, grateful to be able to just sit and be taken somewhere in the warmth of the moment. It was a cold, grey day and looking out the window caused him to shiver involuntarily.

The university looked deserted compared with the normal hustle and bustle, and there was no trouble getting a park right outside the Computer Sciences block. They went into the administration block first as Dave had to collect a few things from his office. As they reached the first floor corridor, the phone began to ring in Dave's office. Fumbling with his keys Dave told Jason to wait for him in the machine room foyer.

Jason knew the way. He had been there often. He wandered through two sets of swing doors and across the covered walkway bridge to the Computer Centre building. From the foyer he could see most of the machine room and adjoining offices through the glass wall partitions. Just behind the first partition he could see the HP plotter, a print-out terminal designed to draw pictures. Once he had seen it in operation and was determined to learn how to program it one day. The room was wide and long, and held numerous tall, metal cabinets. He had learned what most of them were, and had even seen inside some.

The two main computers were fairly distinctive. The Burroughs 9600 was the bigger one – it filled eight cabinets, not counting its tape and disk drives and printers. The Prime 570, on the other hand, was all in one cabinet, and Jason knew that its central processing unit could easily fit inside a suitcase. The Prime had its own tape and disk drives, and with the racks of controllers and printers, the tape library and the adjoining office, this was a very complex room.

Jason's main interest wasn't in these relative giants which could serve up to one hundred remote on-line terminals at once. He had come to test his skills against the new Programming Research Computer. It was an experimental computer recently brought in from overseas and no-one was sure yet exactly how powerful it would be. It had been designed to be virtually self-reprogrammable, and its main purpose was to create and test self-evolving programs, programs that could modify and improve themselves in response to changing demands on data mediums, display modes and computer-to-computer link-ups.

Jason already had a few ideas he wanted to try out, although he did not know yet if he was even going to understand the thing at all. At least in the beginning his father would help him.

When Dave finally arrived, he looked worried.

"Right, come on in, Jase."

The first door took them into the operator workroom. The Operations Supervisor was on duty and two postgraduate students were also there working on the terminals to the mainframe computers.

"Jason, this is Sharon, the Operations Supervisor. I think you may have met before."

"Oh, yes, the computer boy. How are you, Jason?"

"Fine thanks."

"Good to hear. Your dad tells me you've booked time on the PRC."

"Yes, well, he did it really."

"Well, good luck anyway. You're very lucky."

"Thanks. I'll see how I go."

"And over there," continued Dave, "are Steven and Debbie – sorry, Deborah. You may see them around during the holidays. Right. Time's running on, let's have a look at Percy."

"Percy?" Jason queried, puzzled.

They went across to the machine room. "P-R-C, Percy. Get it?" said Dave as he unlocked the smaller room where the new computer was set up.

The Programming Research Computer didn't look much bigger than a normal micro, though the keyboard was more complicated. Jason studied it.

"That's not all," said Dave. "The CPU is in this unit for convenience." He bounced his fist gently on top of the low cabinet on which he leant. "Now, just briefly Jase – the PRC has input facilities from floppy disk here, cassette tape here, as well as normal tape here, and disk here. It can address either the 9600 or the 570 like any normal user . . . "

"This can use the other computers?"

"Yep, if it needs to. And it can output to any of these or via the Prime to any of the printers. You'll be sticking mostly to on-line use, though. If you want to store anything for another session, use this floppy disk. It's one that I'm not using anymore. It's clean. Now – I'll set you up with a user code and show you the entry procedure – it's a bit different . . ."

Jason's half an hour slipped by unnoticed. It was quite tricky programming a computer to reprogram a program, and several times Dave had to study the handbooks. Jason concentrated hard and although he achieved very little he learned a lot faster than his father had expected.

"Professor McArthur," a voice boomed out from behind them. "The time is five minutes past nine. My time is precious!"

Dave and Jason spun around. Dave answered the man casually, though Jason could detect the tension in his eyes.

"Okay, time's up, Jase. You've done very well so far. I've got a meeting now so you'd better catch a bus home. Here, I'll probably be hours." He handed Jason a dollar.

They joined the dark-suited man who was waiting impatiently in the machine room. He was a large man with a tight face and hard, appraising eyes. He carried a slim, square briefcase. Two more serious-looking men joined them in the foyer, and Dave hurried them all along the corridor where he let them in to a conference room. Jason glanced into the room as he passed the open door. Several more people were inside. Some he recognized as being from his father's department and some were strangers. They all stood about anxiously as if expecting something important to begin. As the door closed Jason glimpsed something that stayed in his mind's eye like an afterimage for some time. The dark-eyed man with the icy voice swung his briefcase up onto the table. It was dark green and had a circular symbol embossed on the leather.

That afternoon when Troy arrived home from skating, Jason at last had the opportunity to tell of his adventures in the hot, windy forest of the last century. When he had finished his tale Troy sat quietly for some time, thoughtfully fingering the rimu cones that Jason had returned with.

"So it's true. We'd better warn Dad," he said at last.

"Warn him?"

"Yeah. I think he's in big danger from those COMPLOK guys."

"COMPLOK?"

"Oh, that's right. I haven't told you. Remember Friday night when you went down to Old Shakey's to get the milk?"

"Uh-huh."

"Well I got talking to Dad and he had this green folder. I almost flipped when I saw it — it had the same symbol that I'd seen on those armoured cars in my dream . . . "

"Time jump," corrected Jason.

"Time jump," Troy repeated slowly as though he was considering the implications of the words. "Anyway, Dad told me a bit about it. COMPLOK stands for Computer Link Overlock. They are some sort of computer technology company that want to get a . . . some sort of hook-up . . . "

"Remote terminal access?" tried Jason.

"No, more than that. Computer-to-computer with that new one in Dad's department."

"The Program Research Computer!"

"Yeah, that's it."

"Holy heck!" Jason sat bolt upright. "I saw them this morning! One was a real creepy kind of guy. He had Dad really worried about something."

Troy took a troubled breath, held it for a moment, then released it in a rush. "Something pretty serious is going on, I reckon. Dad must be right in the middle of it, and one day they'll be around here with an army to arrest him. We've got to warn him!"

"When was it, do ya reckon?"

"How far in the future, you mean? Well, I remember it had been raining, but it was fairly warm . . . um . . . oh yeah, and the trees were all in blossom! Spring! This year, next year, or . . ."

Troy's voice faded out.

"Can't guess the year, eh? Just the time of year."

"Mmm. Anyway, it's going to happen," said Troy disconsolately, his heart sinking.

"Not if we can help it!" stated Jason vehemently. "The future hasn't happened yet. We can change it, maybe. We'll warn Dad, he'll tell those guys to forget it and . . ."

"'Penalty points for changing the course of events'" recited Troy.

"The Time Twister," breathed Jason. "That's the clue!"

"It is strange that it's shown up in Moon Base right now, isn't it?"

"Yeah. Really strange. I've got a feeling it's more than just coincidence," surmised Jason.

"I wonder where it came from? Old Shakey doesn't even know it's there, according to whatshisname, you know . . . "

"Mouse."

"Yeah."

"We should be asking ourselves 'when' it came from," suggested Jason.

"When?"

"Remember it said 'Future Products present Time Twister.' Future Products."

"From the future! Wow! Makes sense. I mean anything's possible with that thing."

They sat in silence for a while, until Troy said, "So who's going to talk to Dad?"

"I'm afraid he's not going to believe either of us," said Jason rather doubtfully. "You've got to admit it does sound rather far-fetched. I can't believe it myself sometimes. I think we're going to have to find out a bit more. Maybe look into the future. See what those COMPLOK guys are up to and get some proof to show Dad. Photos or something."

"Yeah," said Troy, unenthusiastically, "risky."

"We've got to do something. Maybe if we could pick up a newspaper to prove we've been there, and . . . "

"What if the Time Twister is part of COMPLOK?"

Jason chewed his lower lip thoughtfully. "No," he said. "If it was, those guards would've known you were arriving. They wouldn't have wanted anyone else to find out their game. It can't be part of COMPLOK."

"You mean, maybe COMPLOK's got enemies?"

"Why not? Oh, I don't know. Look, let's go down to Moon Base about dinner time and have a look at it, at least. No one else will be there at that time of day."

But someone was there. It was their sister, Helena. She was intently involved in playing the Space Invaders machine and didn't see Troy and Jason come in. They watched in growing amazement as she played on and on. Finally she played out with such a high score that her codename went on to the Top Ten list.

The two boys gasped when they saw what she had keyed into the machine: XXX!

"Oh! Hi you guys!" Helena was momentarily startled. "Ha!" She grinned self-consciously at her brothers as they stood gaping at the video screen. "So, I'm found out. Oh well. Ha!" She lapsed into silence.

"Going straight home?" Troy enquired.

"S'pose so. Hey, what's the time?" The two boys looked at their watches.

"Help!" she said when they told her.

"Could you check the stuff in the oven for us? We made something for dinner."

"Yeah, okay."

"We'll be home soon."

"All right. See you later." Helena moved off through the doorway. Moments later they heard the shop door open and close. They turned at last to the Time Twister.

But Helena hadn't left the shop. Instead she idly flicked through a magazine for a minute, then drifted back to the entrance to the games room. The shopkeeper was busy with a customer and the boys were engrossed in the Time Twister. She crept in and hid behind the open door where she made herself comfortable and listened with interest to the boys' conversation.

"If this much is about a hundred years into the past, then the same amount up would be a hundred years into the future."

"So it came from the year two thousand and eighty-six? Wow!"

"Maybe."

"Let's just play a game without the helmet and see."

"Okay."

Jason played. He wove an intricate dance up and down and across the time scale, and over and under the pattern of events.

He played well and Troy was impressed. Finally he ran out of 'Time Jump Reserve'.

"Is that a good score?" Troy asked.

"Not bad. Did you notice the forward jumps only went to forty-eight units on the time scale?"

"Forty-eight years, you reckon?"

"Who knows?" Jason shrugged.

"Nineteen-eighty-six plus forty-eight, that's... ah ... two thousand and thirty-four!"

"Maybe. Hey, look!" Jason pointed at the screen. For a few seconds it said:

JASON
PLEASE
TIME JUMP
FULL FORWARD
WE ARE FRIENDS
WE NEED YOUR HELP

They looked at each other, unable to believe their eyes, hearts racing.

"Did you see that?"

"Sure did."

"Someone's definitely behind it, that's for sure."

"And they know who we are."

"That's bad."

"Why bad?"

"Dunno. I just don't like it, that they know. It's creepy."

Troy wrapped his arms about his chest and nibbled nervously on his lower lip. "What if it's a trap? It might be COMPLOK again. Come on, let's just leave it, eh?"

"Look!"

Once again the usual pattern of the screen was interrupted by a message:

TROY RELAX
WE ARE NOT COMPLOK
WE NEED YOUR HELP

"Okay, okay, I'll relax, although I'm not too sure about this, Jase." He paused to think. "It could be dangerous, I'd better go first." He held a twenty cent piece ready.

"All right," agreed Jason. He knew that Troy was just trying to be the responsible older brother. Grimly Troy inserted the coin and took down the helmet. His hands shook as he put it on.

He was afraid. Memories of his first time jump came rushing back and his stomach lurched. He pushed the control up and hit it. Nothing happened. He tried again. Nothing.

"It doesn't work," he said with relief.

YOU ARE AFRAID
LET JASON TRY

"Okay," Troy answered aloud. "Here you are, Jase, but be ready to come back straight away. Don't leave the machine whatever you do, okay?"

"Okay, sure. I promise I'll be ready. Thanks." He gripped Troy's hand clumsily, then said, "For Dad."

"Right. Good luck."

Jason took a long, deep breath and let it out slowly. That helped a little to settle the butterflies in his stomach. He stood squarely in front of the Time Twister. Troy stood off to one side, his eyes not leaving his brother for an instant.

"I'll be right here," he said reassuringly.

"Thanks. Won't be long, I hope." He grinned suddenly and put the helmet on carefully. He pushed firmly upwards on the control until it stopped. Nothing existed except himself and the machine. A feeling of confidence seemed to flood from it, as if his family were all close around him. He touched the control button.

★ ★ ★

Briefly he felt a sensation like taking an enormous leap, although he knew that he had not moved at all. But now a completely new world surrounded him and the Time Twister. At first it seemed like a jungle but after a few moments he saw it as it really was – a multitude of huge, potted plants in a glasshouse. More details entered his consciousness as he slowly turned about. Glass walls, a whole room filled with tables, cabinets, consoles, screens and more pot plants. He was standing on a kind of grid from which huge, coloured cables snaked away to other machines, and a frame of polished metal rose up about him, capped with a similar grid above his head.

"Jason. Welcome." A man's rich voice greeted him. Stepping out from behind a control desk came a handsome, middle-aged man dressed in a colourful robe and soft boots. Jason stared in amazement because for a moment he had thought this was his own father, but it wasn't. Nevertheless he couldn't shake the feeling that he had met this man before.

Chapter five

The man came up to him, beaming with some inner joy. He extended his hand and said, "Just call me Yos."

Jason hesitated. "Yos?"

"That's right." They shook hands. The man's hand was strong, but gentle and reassuring. His eyes were bright and looked straight into Jason's eyes, not staring, but trustingly. So they stood for a timeless moment, meeting by hand and eye. Jason already felt quite at ease with Yos even though they had met only seconds previously. Once again Jason felt his memory stir, as if this man was already well known to him.

"Jason, you have just undertaken an incredible journey. Although you are still standing on exactly the same spot you were standing on at Moon Base, you are now almost thirty years into your future." Then Yos began to laugh, still looking directly at Jason, until Jason began to feel puzzled and slightly hurt at being laughed at.

"I'm sorry, Jason. This is as incredible for me as it is for you. One day you'll get the joke, if you can call it that." Yos controlled his mirth and continued, "You were brave to use the Time Twister and come so far into an unknown time. I know that you did it for your father's sake, and already you have set off a whole new chain of events."

Jason's attention was caught by the word 'events' and Yos noticed this.

"Have no fear, let's just say for now that your coming here is like riding a Green Event on the Time Twister screen. This place," Yos indicated the whole vast room with a sweep of his hand, "is one of the very few time travel stations on Earth, and you are one of the very few human beings who have the Gift. This place, including the portal-field generators that stand seven levels above us and seven levels below, has been built on this particular spot for you."

Jason was flabbergasted. "For me?"

"Those with the Gift inevitably turn up in very close proximity to crucial nodes in the matrix of historical events."

"Pardon?"

"Sorry. Let me rephrase that. Very soon, in your time, the history of this country, and possibly the world, will take a turn for the worse. You Jason, with help from us here and your own family, can turn the course of those events. You have the Gift."

"What is the Gift?"

"The ability to time travel. Something like what people used to call 'extra-sensory perception', or ESP."

"Yes. I've read a book on ESP."

"However it's not quite the same. We've learned a little about it over the past thirty years, enough to develop this clumsy technology and actually begin to use it to – ah – enhance the survival of the human race, for want of a better description. The ability only seems to occur in children. Once they mature, it disappears. It is very rare. From our computer analysis of history, we've managed to identify only five other nodal realignments . . . "

Yos noted Jason's puzzled look. "Nodal realignments are moments in history when events have been altered by the actions of time travellers. This whole project and others like it were set up to contact and assist these people. Only a few children in our entire history actually come to realize and use the Gift."

"Wow!" Jason's head buzzed with excitement and he was suffused with a secret pride.

"The Gift," Yos stated firmly, as if he could read Jason's mind, "is not a toy. It is bestowed upon you only so that you may serve the people of your land. It is an honour and a burden. Have no fear, Jason. I can tell you now that your task will be successful." Yos gripped Jason warmly by the shoulder and grinned. His friendliness quickly dissolved the doubts and fears that had been forming in Jason's head.

"You have questions," Yos said.

"Yes, can you explain . . . "

"First, come and relax. We have a few

minutes." He led Jason to an alcove among the jungle of indoor plants. They sat down in low, comfortable chairs to hot drinks and biscuits. As Jason sat down, subtle music with a haunting quality seemed to drift from out of thin air. He gave up trying to identify the source and tried the drink before him. It was rich and spicy, not very sweet but rather refreshing. Jason realized he was starving and soon ate all the biscuits while listening to Yos speak. Jason kept Yos busy with an endless flow of questions, yet all the time Yos appeared amused by some private joke.

"Who or what is COMPLOK?" asked Jason.

"COMPLOK is to all appearances a perfectly trustworthy computer business which specializes in computer link-ups. They supply specialized hardware and software including some sophisticated security systems and an armed security guard service . . ."

"What were those guns that Troy saw them shoot Dad with in the future?" interrupted Jason.

"Those were sonic disrupters. COMPLOK has developed them for security duties. They fire a pulse of ultrasonic sound that temporarily affects the nervous system. Anyway, most people that work for COMPLOK are merely innocent employees, but those at the top are a team of international computer criminals, very intelligent and powerful people. Those three that you met this morning, for instance." Jason shivered as he remembered. "They intend to take over your whole country by taking control of all of the main computers in government, banks, police and army headquarters, post offices and big businesses."

"But what's all this got to do with Dad?"

"At the centre of their scheme is what they call the Master Program. It behaves somewhat like a virus, infecting other computers and eventually taking them over, virtually unnoticed."

"Jeez," murmured Jason.

"It is probably the most sophisticated piece of computer fraud ever to be attempted. However – COMPLOK require one more thing. They want to enslave the Programming Research Computer at the university. The Master Program will eventually use the computer's full capacity since it will grow and change itself far too rapidly for any human programmer to keep up with it."

"And Dad's in the way, right?" surmised Jason.

"No. COMPLOK has already gained his approval, as of this afternoon in your time. Nothing stands in their way now. But later, as they establish their network of power, they will start to tidy up a few loose ends. I don't wish to cause you undue anxiety — it need not happen that way."

"But you said before that I – that we – succeed. So how is it Troy saw Dad being taken away?"

"Troy visited one of many possible futures. In that one COMPLOK had succeeded in their takeover. His time trip went into the future most likely to follow your present time. We must work hard to change that likelihood and bring about a better future. Your decision to follow the Time Twister to its origins here has already begun those changes".

"Then this is a less likely future?"

"From your point of view, yes. Think of it this way. Life is like driving down a road with many turn-offs. Once you choose to follow a particular road there is no turning back, and the scenery you see, the people you meet and the adventures you have will all be different from those on another road. Sometimes, no matter which road you take, it keeps turning you back to the one direction. That is your special road which you must follow to its end. The Gift is like that special road but it can also be used to jump around on to any road you wish. Used unwisely you could end up very lost, and countless other people with you. Do you understand what I'm getting at?"

Jason nodded slowly. "Yes. I think so."

"Any other questions?"

"Mmm – how does the Time Twister work? I mean, if it's the Gift . . . " Jason could not quite explain what he was thinking.

"The Gift is the moving force but at this stage it is buried deep in your subconscious. The Time Twister helmet can detect it, and the Time Twister itself coupled with the very powerful portal-field generators here can amplify it until it becomes effective. The Time Twister also helps you at this early stage to focus your willpower so that you can control your time jumps. The bases of these machines are what we call 'bio-synergic circuitry'.

They are grown like plants – in fact they are plants in most respects."

"Plants?" Jason could not comprehend this new piece of information.

"Yes. The time helmet and Time Twister are alive! Plants are extremely sensitive to all life forces and can communicate with each other, even across the barriers of time. That's why all these other plants are here – to keep the Time Twister company. Plants get lonely, you see. They are all in touch across time and space," Yos stated with confidence.

"Across space?"

"Yes, they communicate across space as well. That is where most of the research is being done."

"But I've only travelled in time, haven't I? Not . . ."

"Only in time," Yos assured him. "If you need to go to another place as well as another time, you've got to get there in the usual way before you make the jump."

"Oh!" Jason sat aghast as he thought things through. Finally he asked, "How did the Time Twister get itself into my time?"

"It didn't. Someone has sent it back. Someone with the Gift fully developed. She is close to your age and is actually nearby, but in a special life-support chamber, since she must remain in a trancelike state for the entire project. One day you will meet her." Yos gave him a peculiar look. "Any more questions?"

"So what do I have to do," asked Jason in a small voice, "to help in this project?"

"Not yet, Jason. First you must practise. Practise and observe. Tomorrow I want you to play the Time Twister without the helmet, just game after game . . . "

"But I'll spend all my allowance!" Jason protested.

"Put your left hand on the table, Jason," said Yos putting his own hand out, palm down. Puzzled, Jason followed suit. "Now remember this sequence," and Yos tapped out a short rhythm on Jason's hand: tap, tap-tap, pause, tap-hold, tap, tap. "Repeat it to me."

Jason tapped it out correctly, but Yos insisted on several repetitions before he was satisfied that Jason had memorised it thoroughly.

"Just tap that rhythm on the time-jump trigger of the Time Twister. It's your own private password to as many free games as you want. All right?"

"All right! I'll say!" Jason beamed at the thought. Free games!

"Now, it's time you were off. It's been a very busy evening for you. Now that you're going to be living more than twenty-four hours each day, you must get lots of sleep. You'll need it." Yos stood and led Jason back to the Time Twister platform.

"Play the game and observe. It is designed to teach you the intricate consequences of being able to time travel, and as you play the Gift will be strengthened and brought closer to your conscious centres of control. Don't attempt any more time jumps until tomorrow evening, then return here for further instructions. Ready?"

Jason stepped up to the Time Twister, his mind spinning. There was so much to remember. He noticed then that the Time Twister was not a nebulous holographic image this time but a solid object. He turned to Yos, another question on his lips.

"Enough questions for now," said Yos, reading his mind again.

"Save it for next time. Now – good time travel relies on good imagery, so close your eyes and imagine your own time. Picture Troy standing by the Time Twister. Picture the time. Was the sun setting, or had it already set? Picture your digital watch. Picture the date on a mental calendar that stretches out like a railway track between then and now. A model railway track – and you are big enough to pick up the train from this end and put it at the other end. That is the Gift. It picks you up and moves you whenever you ask it to. But you must have a real desire to be moved. I'll see you soon. Go to your own time now."

Jason opened his eyes and turned. Yos was already at his control panel. They saluted each other in silent farewell, their eyes meeting across the room.

"Concentrate – imagine – ask – " intoned Yos.

Jason turned to his task. Imagining a thirty year

long railway track was very difficult, and instead of imagining himself as bigger he began to feel smaller and smaller, like an ant on an endless railway track. Once again he felt that fear that he might never see his family again. Troy would be forever waiting at Moon Base. An image of Troy standing beside the Time Twister swam into Jason's mind, and with it a longing to be back in his own time. He spoke silently within his mind, "Gift, please take me home."

★ ★ ★

Troy knew it was gone, whatever that mysterious ability had been. He wouldn't time travel again, ever. He was angry with himself for being afraid, and jealous of Jason. He'd blown it — here was something his 'baby brother' could do that he couldn't. He felt powerless but fortunately he did not have long to dwell on his feelings. After touching the control, Jason seemed to flicker for a mere instant, then he was standing still, eyes closed, as if listening to something.

"Jase?" Troy spoke hesitantly.

Jason's eyes jerked open. "It works! It works!" he beamed, leaping all over Troy.

"Hey! Steady on," said Troy trying to get away.

"I've just been — oh! You wouldn't believe it. I mean, oh, where can I begin?" Jason spluttered.

"But you weren't gone at all! At least, I didn't see . . ."

"I've been away for hours! Then I came right back to 'now', see? Right back to 'now', like the game!" Jason shrieked with excitement. Troy was silent. He saw, all right, but it took some seconds.

Jason collected himself at last, then said levelly, "I have just been to thirty years in the future. I met . . ." He stopped suddenly as he realized how loudly he was speaking. He looked significantly towards the doorway. "Can't talk here," he said in a whisper. "It's all really important, but it will have to wait. Come on," and he led the way to the door.

Moments later, Helena wriggled out from her hiding place. After checking to be sure the two boys were gone, she returned to the video games room. She stood for a long time in front of the Time Twister, examining it with a new eye. Finally, the scoreboard displayed itself. The top three places were MUZ, JAS and XXX.

Chapter six

It was going to be one of those days. Jason knew it from the time he woke up late. He was hurrying to gulp down some toast and tea when his father came in in his dressing gown.

"I've still got a thumping headache, Jase. If you want to go down by yourself you can. Get the key from Sharon. Try that video game program of yours but only attempt one modification at a time or you'll lose all track of it. I'm going back to bed," and he shuffled off back to the bedroom, his face grey.

Jason pedalled off on his bike into a cold headwind, and it was well after 8.30 a.m. when he finally arrived at the Computer Centre. The toast he had gobbled down still seemed stuck in his throat and he was feeling quite worked up about being late, his father's headache and the enormity of the time travel business. It didn't help when he saw a COMPLOK van parked outside. Sharon was not around, so he asked Steven about the key.

"To the PRC room? It's not locked," he said.

Jason crossed the machine room and stopped in the open doorway. The room was a mess, or so it seemed at first glance. The panels from several of the cabinets were off and wires and cables snaked back and forth across the room. Some sort of microcomputer in a dark green casing sat on a trolley in the midst of the chaos, and down on his hands and knees beside it was a man in green overalls.

As Jason stood there perplexed the figure on the floor sat back on his heels, yawned widely and began packing away some of the cables and equipment. The man caught a glimpse of Jason as he turned which made him jump involuntarily.

"Good lord! Where did you spring from? Don't creep up on people like that." The man stood up slowly as if his legs were very stiff. Jason immediately noticed the COMPLOK symbol on the left breast pocket of his overalls, and above it a plastic identity card. Beside the small photograph were the words: COMPLOK International. Gavin Broadley. PSI Installation. Code B. CI00342/TI20018.

Jason carefully inspected the man before him, trying to work out if he was 'one of them'. He certainly didn't appear to be. Shorter than average and a bit on the tubby side, the man had thick, curly hair and a big droopy moustache. The eyes looking back at Jason twinkled with amusement. Noticing Jason's scrutiny, the man spoke.

"Hi there. My name's Gavin. And you're . . ."

"Jason." He shook the proffered hand.

"Isn't it school holidays?"

"My father works here and I'm allowed some user time on that," Jason indicated the PRC, "from eight-thirty till nine every morning of the holidays. Ah . . . are you going to be long?"

"Long? Ha! I've been here half the night!" Then he added, rather dubiously, "So you know how to work this thing?"

"Well, I'm just learning really. I can't do much yet."

"Hmm, I see. Well as a matter of fact I haven't quite finished yet, but if you're into computers you'd probably be interested in this. Just a sec, and I'll show you." He quickly picked up tools, unhooked cables and closed up cabinets. "That's better. Now we can see what we're doing. This," he patted a small unit newly fitted alongside the computer keyboard on the table top, "is known as a palm-print lock, or more properly 'Touch-sensitive User Identification System'. We just call it Gypsy, because it reads your palm!" He laughed and Jason politely joined in.

It didn't look very impressive. About the size of a lunchbox but built more like a safe, the Gypsy had a strong lid with concealed hinges. There was, however, no sign of a handle or lock.

"How does it open?" Jason asked.

"With a key, of course," laughed the technician as he pulled from his pocket a big bunch of plastic cards on a key-ring. The cards looked similar to bank cards, and Gavin selected one of these which he then slid along a slot on one side of the tightly-shut lid. The thick lid opened with an electronic buzz and slowly swung back to reveal a dark grey screen that bulged slightly in the middle.

"Take a close look," he told Jason.

Jason bent down and saw that the screen was composed of thousands of miniature cells, almost too small to see. From close up they seemed to sparkle with every colour of the rainbow.

"The screen is sensitive enough to detect every mark and line on your hand. If the whole hand-print, including fingerprints, matches any print on file then Gypsy will permit access. It's a lock, and your hand is the key. Simple! Foolproof too, since no two handprints are the same. COMPLOK will be fitting these all over the place. Even cars will have them one day, so they say. Meanwhile, I have to work all night to get this one installed here, God only knows why." He yawned again. "Oh well, nearly done anyway. Hey – since you're here you can help me do a test run. Hang on a minute."

He selected another key this time and unlocked a narrow panel just beneath the touch-sensitive screen. Turning to the equipment trolley, he tossed the keys onto the top level beside the dark green microcomputer, and began looking for something on the lower level. Jason glanced impatiently at his watch. It was 8:42. He sighed – it certainly was one of those days.

"Right," said Gavin. He had a curious-looking cable in his hands, that looked like a liquorice strap of many colours with long, square sockets at each end. It took him a moment to untangle it then he plugged one end into the palm-print unit.

Without warning the big bunch of keys fell to the floor with a loud jingle. They both looked around. There was no one about, although Jason thought for a moment there had been. The technician scooped the keys up absent-mindedly and wheeled the trolley closer to the desk. He plugged the other end of the cable into the microcomputer and used another key to switch it on. He began punching a sequence of numbers on the keyboard too quickly for Jason to follow, and words tumbled onto the screen.

```
            IDENTIFY 10 SECONDS
                    9
                    8
                    7
GOOD  MORNING  GAVIN
LOG  IN  08:43:07  85/5/15
PACKAGE  PLEASE ?
'GYPSY'  MK  2  GRANTED
FUNCTION  /
F1 GRANTED ACTIVATION SEQUENCE RUNNING
GYPSY SN 100154/597 LOC. U.C.C. P.R.C.
COMPLOK  0001
POWER  OK  I.P.L.  OK
CODE  'A'  USERS  ONLY  'MASTER-PLAN'
NO  REGISTERED  USERS
ACTIVATION  COMPLETE
FUNCTION ?
F3  GRANTED  ALARM  CYCLE  TEST/A
TESTFILE 01  OPEN
CODE  PLEASE
```

"What was your name again?" asked the technician, fingers poised.

"Jason. Jason Mc . . ."

"That'll do."

```
JASON  JASON
CODE  ACCEPT
```

"Put your hand on the sensor, palm flat, and hold it still for five seconds. That's the way." Jason pressed his hand down on the small screen. Surprisingly enough it felt warm to the touch.

```
R/HANDPRINT ONFILE T/01
JASON JASON
REGISTRATION CODE 001/T01/AUTHORITY B
```

"Let's look at it on the big screen, shall we?"

```
VIEW 000/T01 MAG 5
AUTHORITY ?
```

Gavin punched in a quick sequence and the screen filled with a complex pattern of crisscrossed lines. Jason was immediately reminded of a zebra's hide.

"Wow! Is that my hand?"

"Sure is! Got a scar anywhere?"

"Yes." Jason consulted his hand. "Middle finger."

The technician moved the image down the screen until they could see the fingers. The fine scar that Jason had had since he was seven years old showed clearly on the screen.

"Each print requires up to sixteen K's of memory."

"Gee, that's a lot!"

"Yep, it's mostly memory. This model can only file up to six prints. Top security applications. Now . . ." The magnified image vanished, and the screen displayed:

```
ALARM CYCLE TEST/A
STANDARD CORRELATION
PARAMETER ACTIVE
```

"Put your right hand on again."

```
MATCHING HANDPRINT ON FILE
T/01 JASON JASON
ACCESS CYCLE OPEN
```

"Put your left hand on, now."

```
NO MATCHING HANDPRINT ON FILE
ACCESS DENIED
ALARM CYCLE TRIGGERED
ALARM COMPLOK CENTRAL ONLY UNCONFIRMED
★  ★  ★  FAULT-ALARM SIGNAL UNCONFIRMED
★  ★  ★  FAULT TRACED
MODEM 20M/UCC PRC/0001
★  ★  ★  MODEM UNCODED
END TEST CYCLE/A
```

The technician cursed under his breath. Jason knew what that meant – it meant no go for Jason McArthur on the PRC today!

"Broadley! What the hell do you think you're doing?" boomed a voice. Jason and Gavin spun around to face a very angry COMPLOK senior executive who stood at the door. "This is a 'Code A' project! This is a serious breach of security. Who's the kid? This installation was scheduled to be completed by seven-thirty a.m. Why wasn't it?"

Gavin Broadley had turned pale. Before he had a chance to reply the irate executive turned on Jason. "What do you think you're doing, wandering in here?"

"I . . ." Jason began. He was trying to stay calm, safe in the knowledge that he was allowed to be there, but his composure had already been upset by the sudden interruption. What he really wanted to do was run. He didn't like this man who he was afraid might turn violent.

"Broadley – did you file his handprint into the security lock?"

"Y-yes, sir."

"Then erase it right now! As for you, kid, you'd better get lost, all right?"

"Sir, he happens to be . . ."

"I don't care who the hell he is, Broadley. Just get on with your job! He should not be here and you're in serious trouble my friend."

Jason gave the technician a quick look as if to say, 'It doesn't matter,' grabbed his schoolbag and rapidly retreated across the machine room. He knew there was no chance of telling the guy he was allowed to be there when the man was in such a state, anyway. Jason was beginning to feel angry himself now. He didn't like being called 'kid' or being yelled at or not being given the opportunity to explain himself. He just wanted to get away and didn't take any notice of anyone or anything until he reached the door leading outside.

"Pig!" he thought. "Rotten pig!"

As he rode away he went over and over the ugly scene in his mind. He kept thinking of things he could have said instead of running away. An angry lump remained in his throat all the way home.

Headache or not, Dave had to get up. He found Jason in the kitchen, halfway through the breakfast dishes. There was something about the way the boy was thumping things into the drying rack that caused him to ask, "What's wrong, Jase?"

Bit by bit the whole story came out. By the time Jason had finished Dave was angry too.

"Right! I'm going to sort this business out right now!" He picked up the telephone and dialled the Computer Centre. After a few minutes he had gleaned all the information he could from the Operations Supervisor. Then he rang COMPLOK.

"Good morning. Martin Murdoch, please . . . Professor McArthur . . . thank you." He pressed his fingertips against his forehead and temple. Now he knew why he had a headache. Too much stress at work lately. All this COMPLOK business.

"Yes, hello. Professor McArthur here. I understand the program access security system was installed last night? Yes, well I've just received a report that the installation ran over time and a scheduled user was ordered out by COMPLOK security . . .That's right . . . This could constitute a breach of contract. However I am prepared to let the matter pass if I have an assurance from COMPLOK that any further work on the link-up will in no way interfere with normal usage of the PRC as per our agreement.

"Further to that, I understand that Security Supervisor Ferris was overseeing the operation, is that correct? . . . Right. Then may I demand that

Mr Ferris be reprimanded for his heavy-handed behaviour this morning. He had absolutely no right to insult and dismiss the scheduled user the way he did after allowing the installation to run overtime. What's more, I think that Mr Ferris would do well to tender his apologies to the user involved. My department has bent over backwards to suit your needs recently. The least your people could do is to show some good manners to my staff and students if you want our continued goodwill. Thank you."

Dave hung up. "Well," he smiled, "that's cured my headache anyway."

The chief executive of COMPLOK International slowly replaced the dead telephone receiver. He thought for a minute, then flicked a switch on his intercom and spoke into it. "Long Range Security Unit? Put Professor David McArthur on 'the list' please."

Practise. Practise and observe, Yos had said, but Jason had become bored with endless games of Time Twister. It had been fun before lunch, but after two o'clock Muzz Watson and his little crowd had been in and out repeatedly. Although it was an extraordinarily warm day for May, they didn't seem able to find anything to do with themselves and kept going on about how boring the holidays were. Muzz kept trying to borrow money off him, although to judge from the number of ice creams and packets of crisps he was eating Jason knew Muzz must have had enough already.

While the others were there, Jason couldn't take advantage of his free games or he'd be faced with some tricky questions. To the other boys Jason seemed even more distant and guarded than usual so they tended to leave him alone.

Nevertheless, Time Twister had become boring. After a while Jason realized that he could only do so much, the patterns of play were always basically the same, and his scoring seemed to have reached a limit. The helmet remained untouched in its niche and its mere presence was a temptation for Jason. He very much wanted to put it on and go exploring in time but Yos had said not to. He sighed in frustration and turned away from the machine.

Sniff and Mouse were in the shop poring over a book or magazine on the counter. What was so unusual was that Old Shakey was looking at it too and talking about it to the boys. Jason joined them and discovered that it was Old Shakey's photograph album. Mouse had apparently started talking about something in the 'olden days' and the next thing they knew Old Shakey had brought out the photo album. They flipped over the pages.

"What're these ones?" asked Mouse, pouncing on an old envelope full of photographs that was tucked in between the last pages.

"Ah – those!" Bob Shackle deftly retrieved the envelope from the boy's over-eager grasp. "When I bought the shop, these came with it. It's a sort of a photographic record of the place. This one was taken about ten years ago. Not much different really, is it? And this . . . it's written on the back '1953 – additions in progress', but you'll notice that it's a butcher's shop then. Here's another one – butcher's shop again. I suppose that's 'T.C. Tait, Quality Butcher and Co.' standing out the front. Oh, they're all out of order. Here's the earliest one, I think. '1933, Albert B. Lambert, Mrs A.B. Lambert . . .' Look, I'm sorry boys, there are people waiting to be served. Have a quick look then I'll put them away. Take them over there."

The three boys carefully carried the album over to the freezer top and went through them again. Jason was fascinated by the series of photographs of the shop. The 1933 photograph showed only a house, with the family lined up on the footpath outside, eldest to youngest, as they did in those days when they were having a photograph taken. Later on a small shop was built onto the front. Mrs Lambert's Millinery. It was expanded after the war and then became Tait's Butchery. Another bit was built on in 1953, the storeroom which today was Moon Base. That was what fascinated Jason the most, that latest addition. Before 1953 there was a driveway there, and before that there was just lawn behind a neat, white picket fence.

Jason's boredom was replaced by a rising excitement. He knew what he'd do. He carefully studied the old brown photograph before putting it away with the others and letting Mouse return it with lots of 'Thank-you-very-muches' and 'That-was-very-interestings'.

"Jase, we're going down the creek. Wanna come?"

"Oh, yeah. I'll come down later, maybe."

"Suit yourself," said Sniff a little coldly, and he rode off with Mouse towards the Manor Road bridge.

Jason didn't notice the snub. Within moments he was back at the Time Twister. Without hesitation he tapped out the familiar rhythmic code and the machine lit up. Putting the helmet on, Jason experienced an intoxicating sensation of great power. He felt like some kind of giant capable of many things. He now felt much more aware of the Gift, and was sure that the jump to 1933 would be easy. No harm could come of it, surely.

After glancing around once more to ensure no one was watching, Jason fixed the image of the old photograph in his mind and imagined himself going back through the years until he reached 1933. Then he jumped.

★ ★ ★

This time he had anticipated the drop from the floor level to that of the ground and landed lightly on his feet. He looked around quickly. No one had seen him arrive – that was just how he wanted it to be. The Time Twister floated in a semi-transparent state in the air. Before he returned he would have to pile something up to stand on, or else he would arrive back at Moon Base buried in the floor! The Time Twister image was his guide to the correct height. First, however, he decided to have a quick look around. He'd only taken two steps when he heard a soft thump, and a girl's voice, "Oof!" He spun around and gasped at what he saw.

"Helena!"

Chapter seven

Helena sat in a crumpled heap in the lush, summer grass and looked up at Jason.

"Hi!" she said, quite naturally. "Just look at this neat place, will ya?" She jumped up and ran lightly to the white picket fence where she stood gazing down the street. Old-fashioned houses that looked new, spindly little trees, and wooden lampposts with lights on them that looked like clown's collars. Across the street, instead of a row of shops, were green fields.

Jason followed her to the fence. He noticed that she was wearing a time helmet too. "You can't just . . ." he began.

Helena turned and looked past him. "Oh, look! How does it stay there?" She ran back to the shimmering shape of the Time Twister and walked all around it, fascinated. Finally she turned to Jason. "How does . . ."

"How did . . ." began Jason simultaneously. He felt alarmed by this sudden turn of events, most of all by the fact that she also had a helmet on, and he knew there was only one. Anger boiled up inside him, a selfish anger because his sister had also penetrated the secret of the Time Twister. His secret.

Helena was staring at his helmet. She reached up to touch her own and her eyes lit up with a sudden realization. Jason took a deep breath, trying not to lose his cool. "Look, Helena, you can't just . . . "

"Who are you?" challenged a girl's voice off to the side of them. The two time travellers spun around to see a girl in fancy dress standing at the corner of the house. She glared at them. "Well?" she asked.

"Hi, I'm Helena and this is my brother Jason," said Helena quickly, moving towards the girl. "We've just arrived – from – er – another town."

"What are you doing in Lambert's yard, then?" demanded the girl. From the corner of the house Helena could see the entire back yard, and noticed two faces peering out the window of the garden shed. Jason nervously glanced at the Time Twister, now appearing very faint in the bright sunlight. Everything seemed to be going haywire and he was considering making a run for it.

"We came to see if we could play," stated Helena boldly.

"Who are they?" called one of the girls from the shed.

"They're on your lawn," answered the first girl. The shed door opened and the other two girls emerged. They were in fancy dress, too. Flamboyant Victorian hats and shawls were draped over prickly-looking, black school gym frocks.

"Shall we tell Mum?" said one of the girls.

"No," said the other, obviously the older sister.

Jason suddenly recognized them from the old photograph. "You must be Mary and Elizabeth Lambert," he blurted out.

"How do you know?" the eldest girl, Mary, turned to Jason.

"He must be from the McArthur's!" said the first girl.

"Haven't seen you before," said Mary suspiciously.

"We're from out of town," repeated Helena.

"What town?" Mary asked.

"Avonfield," replied Jason automatically.

"This *is* Avonfield!" the three girls chorused, looking at Jason as though he was a bit simple.

"We come from the Avonfield of the future," Jason announced bluntly. Helena threw him an anxious glance, not at all sure that he was doing the right thing.

"The future, huh?" said Mary, doubtfully.

"Poppycock!" the younger girl burst out. "Poppycock and bull!" The other two girls began to giggle at this outburst and Helena joined in their mirth. Miffed at being called a liar, Jason pulled a coin out of his pocket. It was a twenty cent piece dated 1981.

"Look at this, then. It's proof, see?" The girls examined the coin with interest, and Helena gave her brother another warning look.

"It's the same size as a florin," said one.

"Who's Elizabeth eleven?" said one of the others.

"Twenty? It can't be worth a whole pound!" said the third.

"That's the Queen," said Jason. "Elizabeth the second."

"No such person!" Elizabeth Lambert stated flatly.

The two older girls began whispering, and soon all three retreated to the shed for a very animated, hushed conversation. Helena took the opportunity to have a quick word with her brother. "Don't tell them any more about the future, understand?" she hissed.

"Why not?" reacted Jason huffily. "It can't hurt."

The girls returned, smiling mischievously. "If you come from the future, you must know what's going to happen, right?" began Mary.

"Well . . . yes, I s'pose so," ventured Jason hesitantly.

"So you'd already know who we're going to marry, wouldn't you?"

"Well, I . . . look . . . " stammered Jason.

"So does Abbie marry Tommy Tait or Willie McArthur?" Mary asked quickly.

Her friend blushed instantly, and tried to gag Mary with her hand, saying, "Mary! You said . . . " She was lost for words in her acute embarrassment. Helena was not, however. She suddenly turned to the girl named Abbie.

"What's your full name?"

"Abigail Eileen Patterson," the girl said quietly. Helena went pale and grabbed Jason by the sleeve.

"Quick, Jase, it's time to go."

"What for?" he protested as they drew closer to the Time Twister on the front lawn. He'd been all ready to announce that Tommy Tait would be the one and that this place would be a butcher's shop and so on, and couldn't understand Helena's sudden panic.

"You know!" Mary screeched after Helena. "You know who it'll be, don't you? You're a witch!" The girls followed them around the side of the house like a pack of hunting wolves. Jason managed to break free of Helena's grasp and ran back for a big, old, metal tub he had observed earlier to be leaning against the back of the house.

"Jason!" yelled Helena, not understanding what he was doing. "Come on!" She was scared. Mary had developed an unnerving expression and was watching Helena like a snake, breathing, "You know, you know," over and over again.

Jason came racing back as fast as he could, the metal tub banging against his legs as he ran. The Lambert sisters let out a howl of protest when they saw the tub. So did Helena, but it was the noise it was making that worried her. Jason flung the tub at the base of the Time Twister image and at last Helena understood. "Not high enough," she observed and sped off towards the fence. She picked up two bricks from amongst the weeds and was back within seconds.

Somewhere a door opened. "Elizabeth! Mary!" a voice called.

"You're in for it now," Elizabeth spat at Helena, who was scrambling up to balance on the two bricks on top of the upturned tub. "Mum! Come quick!"

Jason was yelling instructions but Helena ignored him. She turned to Abbie saying, "I'm sorry, Abbie. I do know but I can't tell you. It could change everything. Marry the man you really love." Helena seemed to grasp at mid-air then vanished. The three girls fell back in astonishment.

"Here! What are you doing, boy?" An irate Mrs Lambert was marching across the lawn towards Jason. Jason wasted no time in leaping up onto the bricks. Wobbling perilously for an instant, he too disappeared.

★ ★ ★

Jason stood shaking for a full minute following his return. Who would have thought that three girls playing dressing-up could suddenly have seemed so threatening? The whole visit had been completely crazy right from the very start. And Helena! She was using the Time Twister too. That would surely muck everything up for him. How did she get the helmet when he already had it? And what on earth was all the fuss about with Abbie and her future husband? It was strange that they mentioned the McArthur name a couple of times . . . Willie McArthur.

It came to him with an almost physical jolt —

Willie McArthur was his grandfather, his father's father. That was it!

Abigail Eileen Patterson . . . oh no! He turned pale and felt weak at the knees. Old Abbie McArthur. Nanna. No! Not possible. His own grandmother! She'd died before he could really remember her. Oh no! And he was about to tell her she would marry Tommy Tait! What if she had?

Jason fled from the shop. He ran as though he was being pursued by a hundred devils. No one was there to notice except Helena.

She had been watching the shop for some time and as soon as Jason was out of sight, she went straight in and slid twenty cents into the slot of the Time Twister machine. Putting on the helmet, she stood silently with her eyes closed for several seconds. Then, she decisively pulled the time-jump control downwards. As if guided by some inner sense, she chose her moment and touched the trigger, her eyes still closed in intense concentration.

Had anyone been watching, Helena would have appeared to have suddenly staggered a little as if overcome by a momentary dizziness. It took her longer to regain her inner equilibrium however. The brief and unexpected encounter with her father's mother as a young girl had completely unnerved her. She now understood the incredible, dangerous power of time travel and was not sure that she could cope with another emotional shock such as that she had just experienced. But her instincts told her she had to move into the future, to where Jason had been, and that it was now or never.

Swiftly she pushed upwards on the control . . .

★   ★   ★

"Just call me Yos," said the tall, graceful woman who stepped down from the computer console. "I have been expecting you. You have just had a disturbing lesson in time travel. Would you like to talk to me about it?"

Helena heard a distant voice answer, "Yes" and realized it was her own. Her mind was actively trying to take in her new surroundings and the woman called Yos. She looked so familiar, yet somehow Helena couldn't place where or when she knew her from. "May I sit down?" she asked.

"Certainly," said Yos and led her to the same seat in which her brother had sat.

★   ★   ★

Once again Helena seemed to flicker in front of the video game, then she quickly removed the helmet and replaced it in its cradle. The lights within the semi-transparent plastic cabinet went out but then something quite new happened. As if by magic a hole appeared in the machine at about Helena's knee-level. She reached in without hesitation and withdrew an identical helmet. Tucking it beneath her arm she quickly walked out of the shop. Once outside she fished a newspaper out of a rubbish receptacle and carefully wrapped the helmet in it. She glanced around furtively then headed towards home. The wind was from the northwest now and was pleasantly warm. It stirred up the autumn leaves and sent them swirling across the road, piling up in deep drifts against nearby fences. Helena hugged the bundle to her chest and moved through the leaves as if in a world of her own.

Safe in her bedroom she gently unwrapped the helmet and examined it carefully, mulling over in her mind what Yos had said about it. It was a plant – a living thing genetically engineered and grown to tune in to her own brainwaves to link her to the Time Twister, which was also a kind of plant computer. It was so utterly fascinating! Helena longed to know more about it and resolved there and then to study biology at High School.

And the Gift! She had the Gift! Her mind swam with a multitude of thoughts and she felt years older than she had done that morning. If only there was someone that she could talk to about it. Not for the first time did she wish that Natty was home. Carefully she hid the helmet among her house plants and curled up on the bed.

She must have fallen asleep. Suddenly she was aroused by a quick knock on her door and Troy and Jason walked in. Each had a determined look on his face, and Helena immediately guessed that they had come to have a serious talk with her. Troy began at once.

"Helena. There's something very important going on. Dad's in danger and Jase and I are trying to do something about it. It concerns the computers at the university and some guys who are trying to carry out a major takeover. Anyway, it's all pretty risky, and we think it'd be best if you don't fool around with the Time Twister anymore." Helena gasped with indignation. She rose up to make an angry retort when Troy continued. "It really does work, as you've discovered. Only certain special people can use it. It seems that all three of us have an ability. But it's not a toy. Time travel can have dire consequences."

Jason stood staring at the floor. Helena was still red with rage but held back her planned outburst.

"It's the key to the whole plan so we can't risk mucking it up. It's far too important."

Helena had remembered something. One of the many things Yos had told her during her two-hour visit to the future was that this very confrontation would take place and how she must handle it. So, despite her anger she simply said, "Okay, I won't fool around with the Time Twister anymore." She gave Jason a dirty look nonetheless. "Is Dad home?"

"Yeah, he's cooking dinner."

"I think I'll go and give him a hand."

Her father turned as she strode angrily into the kitchen. "Oh, you're home! I thought you were still over at Miriam's. Did you see the parcel?"

Helena's heart leapt. "What parcel? From Mum?"

"Yes. Didn't the boys tell you? It arrived this afternoon."

"No they didn't, the bums!"

"Hey, hey, hey! Steady on, girl, that's a bit strong!"

"Well they are!"

"Why? What have they done now?"

"Aw, nothing. What's in it? Have you opened it?"

"I've been waiting till everyone was here," said Dave. "Go and get the boys and we'll open it together."

"I'd rather take the compost bucket out. It's nearly full."

"Uh-huh, I see. Okay, I'll get the boys."

The parcel was from Natty, of course, and contained a huge tapa cloth which they promptly hung on one wall of the living room. There was also a packet of photographs, and in the accompanying letter she announced that she would soon get some leave to come and visit them all again. They talked about it all during dinner, though Jason seemed quieter than usual.

Later on Jason sneaked out the back door. It was still warm and the wind had died down so he decided to walk to Moon Base. He had a lot to think about. So Helena had the gift too. She really messed up his little trip to 1933. How did she manage to find him? She'd better not try it again. If she followed him on the COMPLOK mission . . . he decided not to mention it to Yos.

Without hesitation Jason time-jumped to the future. It was becoming easier and more natural to him every time. Yos was there to meet him. "How was your practice today? Did you observe the complex nature of time travel?" Yos asked.

"Uh-huh. It was a pretty interesting day," said Jason, truthfully.

Yos gave him a searching look and Jason had to look away. "What do I do now?" he asked, gazing around the Time Travel Station.

"Practise," replied Yos. "The success of your mission against COMPLOK relies on accurate time jumps. Accurate to within seconds. Do you think you can do that?"

"Yes, of course I can," said Jason, with more conviction than was necessary.

"Well, we'll see. Here's your homework. This is a list of twenty precise times, all on different dates with different time-jump intervals. Go to the Post Office where you can see through the window a clock and a calendar to check yourself against. Do the practice jumps there, in the sequence listed."

Jason was puzzled. "How can I do time jumps away from the Time Twister?"

"From now on you will have your own helmet. Now that the Gift has fully surfaced you can use it to jump from any place you want. The controls on the Time Twister were only there to give you an external focus for your unconscious ability. They never really did anything."

"Really?" exclaimed Jason incredulously. "I thought they did!"

"Exactly." Yos smiled. "The Time Twister tricked you into developing the Gift. Nevertheless it is still vital to your work. It acts as an anchor to your own time. Without that you would cease to know where you were in time and become hopelessly lost." At these words a shiver ran down Jason's spine. "Close your eyes, Jason. Become aware of the time helmet. Feel it linking you to the Time Twister even now. Feel your anchor in your own true time. That is your lifeline. Feel it?"

After a moment's pause, Jason nodded and opened his eyes.

"Good. Always be aware of that. It is the starting point for all your time jumps. It is essential that you return to your own time or the entire matrix of events will be disrupted. History will change. For similar reasons, your mission against COMPLOK must be done as close to your own time as possible. The repercussions of one small but unwise action can be enormous. Do you understand that now after today's work?"

Jason didn't look up. "Yes, I think so." He had a feeling that somehow Yos already knew about his visit to 1933. At least he wasn't making a big deal out of it as some adults would have done.

"Good. Now, here's your helmet. Remember, this is a living thing and it must be cared for as such. Do you have any houseplants in your room? It will need company . . ."

★　★　★

The boy crossed the street from the brightly-lit shop to the Post Office. All the other shops were closed and the street was almost deserted. He went into the foyer and peered through the glass doors. He put a strange-looking hat on his head, then seemed to flicker.

Chapter eight

"Where've you been, Jason?" asked Dave McArthur when Jason walked into the lounge. "Don't just wander off like that, it worries people. Not that I was worried, but it's good manners to tell your old man that you're going down to Moon Base after dinner."

Jason jumped at the mention of Moon Base and Dave's curiosity was aroused. "What's the big attraction at Moon Base these days, anyway? A new video game, I s'pose."

"Well, yes, there is a new one. Everyone's getting into it. I just went down for some practice, that's all."

"Practice? When's the big event?"

"Eh?" Jason was startled by the question. What did his father know? "What d'ya mean?"

"Well you must be practising for something! I assume it's a big play-off, you know – all the gang competing for the top slot and wasting all their money in the process."

"Oh, yeah. We haven't decided yet – maybe Friday."

"And what's it called this time, this new machine?"

By now the television was playing to itself, as both Troy and Helena watched Jason anxiously. Jason caught their eyes briefly, then looked directly at his father to see his reaction. "Time Twister."

"Time Twister?" Dave chuckled. "What next? You'd be better off learning to program them than playing on them, Jase. By the way – sorry about the muck-up this morning but it's all sorted out now. I've got a special security pass for you, compliments of COMPLOK, as well as an apology. Things will be a little strange down there for the rest of the week. Security guards day and night until they've loaded their master program. Supposed to be tomorrow, they reckon. Damned stupid affair if you ask me, it's not our business to aid their research, still . . . oh, did you get your homework?"

Jason's heart lurched. "What homework?" he asked cautiously.

Dave didn't notice his son's nervousness. "I've photocopied the manual for the PRC for you. It's on your bed. Give it a good read through if you want to get anywhere on that computer."

"Oh, thanks. I'll check it out now. Goodnight everyone!"

"Goodnight?" exclaimed Dave in a surprised tone. He glanced meaningfully at his watch. It was only a quarter to eight.

"I've had a big day," Jason told him, knowing that it wasn't a lie.

The sleep had been good, but Jason was now wide awake. He lay in bed considering the peculiar events of the past few days, and a squirming feeling began in his stomach — like an uneasy worm, twisting this way and that in time with his thoughts. Although it was still early, he got up and tried to bury the worm under a big breakfast.

That morning he arrived on time. A COMPLOK security guard examined his pass in the foyer then let him go in. Another guard sat right outside the PRC room. The guard rose and examined the pass again, then spoke into his walkie-talkie. "Jason McArthur, pass number 1818072. Eight-thirty a.m."

The guard motioned Jason to go in, and watched his actions for a time through the window before resuming his seat. Jason muddled about for a while before he managed to get any sense from the computer, then loaded a program of his own that he had on cassette. It was a game that had taken him weeks to program. He had arrived at the idea from swatting flies. Using the graphics package he programmed the PRC to add colour to the picture. That worked, but when he tried to give shadows to the 'flies' he seemed to lose everything.

By nine o'clock he had finally got shadows in, but then the program treated the shadows like the real thing and the game became impossible to play. He left feeling frustrated, but not before noticing that more changes had occurred in the room. COMPLOK must have been working through the night again, setting up the link that the University had never intended.

The day was strangely still. The early morning sun had faded behind a vast cloud cover, a turbulent looking sky in shades of purple and grey. It sat like a heavy lid on Jason's spirit.

Jason went home but found the place deserted, so he picked up his time helmet and left again. He felt troubled. His time-jump practice at the Post Office hadn't gone well so far. He had only done about fifteen on the list as he had felt tired, and it was because of this, he'd reasoned, that his time jumps had begun to go wildly astray. Some had even been whole years off target.

Consequently he repeated all the jumps at another Post Office, since he didn't fancy the idea of bumping into himself at the Manor Road branch. It was an interesting list that Yos had given him. Nearly all the times set down were at night or on Sundays. He supposed this made it easier to avoid people. One sequence involved jumping backwards and forwards through one night. Another took him to many different months and times during 1963 and 1964. He did not know why.

Jason worked steadily through the list. He had certainly improved, as more often than not he was just a minute or two off target though there was still the odd occasion when he was way off course. He felt that his timing was not too bad, so he wandered off to the playground to kill time watching the young children playing on the swings and slides.

He was waiting – waiting for a storm to break. Waiting for COMPLOK to make their move. The sky was also waiting. It hung over him, brooding, like an upside-down world of grey hills and purple valleys. Jason felt restless. If only he could do what he had to do and get it over with. The Gift seemed to weigh on him like the sky. He wished he didn't possess it. Why me? he thought. Why do I have to go through all this?

With a frustrated sigh Jason rose to his feet, making the decision to visit Yos straight away. It wouldn't make any difference anyway, time was flexible.

Arriving at Moon Base, however, Jason found the gang was all there so he couldn't use the Time Twister or his helmet. The gang found him moody and uncommunicative, while he thought they were particularly noisy and uncouth. He drifted away to return later when they had gone.

No one was in the video parlour when Jason returned. Quickly he unfastened his small back pack and withdrew his helmet. Within moments he was thirty years in the future.

★ ★ ★

Yos greeted him warmly, and insisted that they relax and have a cup of tea together before discussing serious matters.

"I suppose you're tired of waiting, Jason," he

said. Jason nodded silently. "How was the practice? Do you think you are good enough to put your ability to the test?"

"Yes, I'd like to get on with it. I think I'm ready."

"Accurate?"

"Yes." Jason knew that wasn't strictly true, but he really did want to get started and felt sure everything would be all right on the day.

"Good. I'll instruct you on your first task right now. Come with me." Yos rose from the seat amongst the jungle of monitors and computer consoles. Jason followed as Yos opened a door and walked into a room that set Jason's mind reeling. It was exactly like the PRC room at the Computer Centre! Yos laughed good-naturedly at Jason's expression of surprise.

"Welcome to my little museum. This," he gestured to the computer, "is the very same one that you were working on this morning. It's almost a museum piece now. All these peripherals are identical to those set up in your time, except for this one. It's a later model but that won't matter. It took me months to find some of this old stuff."

Jason glanced back through the door. "Is all that the very latest in computer technology?" he asked, indicating the Time Travel Station.

"Oh, no. Most of it is nearly fifteen years old but it's good enough for our purposes. Modern computer science has taken an entirely new direction since then. That helmet you are wearing is one of the latest advances. Computer usage is very different in this century, but I'll say no more. You'll see it all come about in time. Now then. Your task tomorrow morning is to take COMPLOK'S tape out of this tape drive here. Have you used one of these?"

"No."

"Right, I'll show you how. . ."

★ ★ ★

Minutes after Jason left Moon Base, the sun shone through below the edge of the bank of clouds and the city and hills were lit as if by a searchlight. The afternoon warmed up a little and Jason's spirits lifted considerably. It was all go now, and success was assured. Carefully Jason went over the instructions in his mind one last time.

As Jason approached the final guard, the man glanced at his security pass and greeted him cheerfully, "Good morning, Jason. May I have a look in your bag, please?" Smiling pleasantly he took the small back pack from Jason's paralysed fingers and unzipped it. "What's this?"

"Ah . . . it's my BMX helmet – for bike-riding, you know." Jason shrugged and tried to smile nonchalantly.

"Yeah, my boy's into track riding too. You might know him – Peter Verseck?" The guard continued to rummage in the bag.

"No, can't say that I do."

"Hmm. Well, that all seems okay. Have a good day."

"Thanks."

"Funny looking helmet for BMX though, isn't it?"

"Ah, yeah. Dad got it for me overseas."

Jason slipped through the door and closed it gently. The guard settled back into his chair to watch Sharon across the machine room. Jason squatted on the floor as if to open his bag. He slipped out the helmet and put it on, keeping one eye on the window. The guard didn't stir. Taking a deep breath to ease the nervousness in his stomach, Jason prepared to time-jump. He formed a mental picture of the target time, 11.32 p.m. Thursday, and reached out with the Gift to that time.

★　★　★

It was quiet and only the night-lights were on. He stood up slowly, then froze. Across the machine room he could see people in the foyer. They were only just leaving! He was too early! The guard was locking the door to the operator workroom and turned just as Jason was about to duck out of sight. Jason was too slow and the guard spotted him. Obviously shocked at seeing Jason there, the guard stood gaping incredulously for a couple of seconds.

Jason didn't waste any time. He leapt to the tape drive cabinet and touched a button. The glass panel began to slide slowly down. Too slow – and the tape required rewinding. There wouldn't be time! The guard was fumbling at the door he had just locked. Jason hit the rewind button as soon as he could reach it and the tape reel began to spin at high speed. Now the guard was through the first door and was unlocking the next one. The others in the foyer had also noticed the disturbance and they were coming too. One grabbed a telephone and began dialling.

The tape was still far from being completely rewound when Jason panicked. He opened the door just as the guard came through the one opposite. "Hey you!" called the guard. "Come back! You can't escape!"

Jason ran around the room behind the huge Burroughs 9600. The guard moved to head him off and as he did so Jason immediately doubled back into the PRC room. The tape was rewound. He wrenched it off the spindle with such force that he stumbled backwards and collided heavily with the guard as he burst into the PRC room. He twisted free, but the guard managed to get hold of the tape. Jason abandoned it and hurtled through the doorway. Two more guards were waiting for him. The primal instinct to escape overwhelmed him and he time-jumped wildly into the past.

● ● ●

He fell forwards, tripped over his feet and banged his shins painfully. His hands crashed into hard bars of steel and there was a sharp, stabbing pain in his palm. Bright daylight, cold air, roaring noise and the smell of rust and wet concrete surrounded him. His head struck a wooden edge and the helmet sprang off. He could feel the cold air on his bare head. Dazed, confused and in pain he struggled up to see where it had gone, but all he saw over the edge were trucks pumping wet cement down a long hose into deep boxing, and workmen in big, rubber boots shouting to each other.

The helmet was down there somewhere, buried under tonnes of wet concrete. He was trapped!

Chapter nine

It was a nightmare. He had woken up but he was still dreaming and now the nightmare was worse than before. All around him workmen were busy building the Computer Centre. It was bitterly cold despite the sunshine. He stood up to attract the attention of the concrete workers beneath him. He wanted to shout, "Stop! Wait! I dropped something in there!" but his voice was caught somewhere between his sinking stomach and his choked-up throat. He was shaking uncontrollably and his bleeding hand stung with pain.

"Oi! Get off there, kid!"

A mass of faces turned up towards him. One man was shouting and gesturing angrily at him, and another was moving towards him across the oiled planks and criss-crossed steel.

"I dunno how you got up here son, but if I were you I'd clear off pretty smartly! What's the matter?" The carpenter was now close enough to see Jason's hand. "C'mon, give us a look, then! Ah, you silly young fool. We'd better get that hand seen to." He led Jason off to the 'smoko' hut.

Jason tried to explain about the time helmet lost in the concrete but there was so much noise he couldn't make himself heard. Once they were inside the hut and the carpenter had cleaned up the shallow, jagged cut on his hand, he finally succeeded.

"What did ya say it was again?"

"A helmet, a sort of crash helmet." Jason angrily brushed the tears away, annoyed at himself for crying.

"Are you Jason?" interrupted a burly, red-faced man who poked his head through the door. It was the same man who had gesticulated angrily at him before. He was very abrupt and unsympathetic, and obviously still angry.

"Yes," admitted Jason in a small, surprised voice.

"Someone here for you," he grunted. Puzzled, Jason moved to the door. Standing nervously behind the workman was a familiar figure clutching a very familiar object. It was Helena.

"I've got it," was all she said as she handed him the helmet.

Jason was completely dumbfounded. As if from a great distance he heard his own voice say, "Thanks". She smiled, and looked with concern at his bandaged hand and tear-streaked face.

"Is that it?" asked the carpenter.

"Yes." Jason turned back to face him. "Uh, thanks." He waved his bandaged hand vaguely. Everything seemed like a movie to him.

The foreman, 'Burly', gave them both a good telling off for fooling around on the building site, warned them never to do it again and suggested they get back to school before he called the police.

"Come on, Alan," he said, turning to the carpenter, "back to work. How the hell did he get up there anyway?"

"Beats me," shrugged Alan, as the pair wandered back on to the site. The last thing Jason and Helena heard before they left was Burly saying, "I'm sure I saw the girl over there too. Didn't you?"

Brother and sister walked for a while in silence. Around them stretched flat fields and the occasional shady, bare tree. Only a few of the university buildings had been built as yet. Frost still lay in the shadows.

Finally Jason found his voice. "Thanks, Helena," he mumbled. Suddenly the full impact of his blunder hit him with force – the mission had failed! COMPLOK would go ahead and the wrong future would come to pass. But Yos had said it would succeed! He felt confused and depressed. There might still be hope; he could warn Dad . . . A jumble of thoughts tumbled about in Jason's mind as they walked. Helena broke the silence.

"I'm glad Yos sent me. I knew you were in trouble, but I couldn't find you at Moon Base, so I went to Yos who told me you were at the Computer Centre. I biked down here . . . "

"How do you find me?" Jason remembered the 1933 shambles.

"It's just a feeling. I follow the feeling – it's part

of the Gift I suppose. Can't you do that?"

Jason didn't answer. Instead he said, "What about the helmet?"

"That wasn't easy. I arrived at the same time you did, but out in the car park. I first saw you on your way down with that man. So I jumped to this evening and climbed up . . . gee, it's cold! Let's find a warmer time. Follow me!" She vanished.

"Hey! Wait a minute!" By the time Jason had put his helmet on she was back.

"Sorry. I forgot you're different." She leaned forward until their helmets touched and took his uninjured hand in hers.

"Just jump forward with me. I'll choose the time. One, two, three . . ."

• • •

Jason had no time to think, he just did it and it worked. It was hot and the sun was high. The air was filled with summer smells. He sneezed. So did Helena. They both laughed and everything felt wonderful.

As she steered him back towards the building site Helena continued her story, "So when I saw no helmet up top, I went back and watched you arrive."

"Did you?"

"Yeah. It was awful. I couldn't do anything, you were so close to the edge. So I time-jumped around a bit till I managed to catch the helmet. It wasn't easy. You should have seen the look on Fatso's face when I asked for you!"

"He must have seen you."

"Yes he did. Twice." Helena laughed. "Boy, was he mad! Where did you start from, Jase?"

"Huh?"

"Where did you time-jump from?"

"Oh, in the PRC room."

"You'll have to show me . . . oh, blast! They've got the doors on already." By now they had reached the building again. It was in a much more advanced state of construction. The doors were in and shut tight.

"Where is everybody?" asked Jason.

"It's Sunday. C'mon, we'll go back a couple of weeks." Once again they touched helmets. This time Jason was ready for it and together they leapt back two weeks in time.

●　●　●

Now there weren't any doors. They walked in to the dim interior and picked their way through the clutter of timber off-cuts and scaffolding. It was damp inside, and smelled of fresh concrete. Jason quickly got his bearings and led the way upstairs to the open space that would one day become the machine room. There were no internal walls built at that stage, so they time-jumped forward a week at a time, Sunday to Sunday, until Jason recognized the layout and found the room where he had begun his ill-fated adventure. The room was empty so he had to guess where he had been crouching down so long ago in the future. He laid out several sheets of thick cardboard, in case the floor level had changed.

"I'll see you soon, Jase. I'd better find my bike before it's pinched. See ya!" She disappeared.

Jason was alone again. He crouched down and focused on the inner link to his own true time. It was still there, as strong as ever. Never had he appreciated the Gift as much as he did in that moment. He relaxed and the Gift took him back to 'Now'.

★ ★ ★

He was not quite in the right place, but it didn't matter. Quickly he stuffed the helmet into his pack and stood up. The guard hadn't moved. Beyond the door the computers and tape drives hummed loudly as always. He sat at the PRC keyboard but did nothing for half an hour except think, and feel more and more depressed.

It was a wild and windy day and unusually hot for May. Dave McArthur was in the garden pulling up the last of the tomato plants. Troy was in the garage dismantling his bicycle. No one saw Jason arrive home. He went and curled up on his bed, staring at the wallpaper. Nobody bothered him for a couple of hours and he didn't move once. Finally

Troy and Helena gently roused him.

"Dad's made lunch. Are you all right?"

"S'pose so," said Jason dully.

"Helena's filled me in on what happened," said Troy. "What were you doing? Is the mission on?"

"Yos sent me to get COMPLOK'S tape. I blew it." Jason lapsed into silence.

"How?"

"I didn't time my jump right, did I!" Jason exploded. "The mission is wrecked!" He threw his arms about angrily then turned and stared out the window.

Helena quietly unzipped his pack, retrieved Jason's time helmet and gently tucked it amongst the house plants on the window sill. "Yos wants to see you this afternoon," she said softly. "C'mon, Dad's waiting."

Head down, Jason slouched out of the bedroom. Troy held back. "Helena," he began, "look – I'm sorry about what I said on Tuesday. You've got the Gift, not me. Well not anymore, anyway, and it looks like you're needed for the mission. The Time Twister is for you, so go for it," Troy finished clumsily.

"I already am!" Helena grinned. "Thanks. I'll forgive you, even if you are a boy."

"What!"

"How does it feel to get a taste of your own medicine, eh?" She wrinkled her nose at him, then grinned again.

"Hey!" their father yelled. "Come on, you guys!"

Jason didn't want to go. It meant reporting his failure to Yos. But what else could he do? Besides, he began to suspect that Yos knew more than he let on. If he knew what was to happen, why did he send him off like that? And why did he tell him it would succeed? Jason's gloom turned to indignation, then confusion. He went.

★ ★ ★

The Time Travel Station was deserted. "Yos?" Jason called softly. "Yos?"

"Jason. You are just in time." Yos stood in the doorway of the duplicate PRC room. "Come in."

Jason went and sat in the swivel chair in front of the computer. Yos took a similar chair. At last Jason met the gaze of the mysterious man. Jason's eyes smouldered with anger and distrust, hurt and confusion. Slowly Yos lowered his own eyes. For a moment he looked small and sad, then he spoke.

"Jason, you deserve an explanation. I'm sorry it had to be this way, but your choices set off an inescapable course of events. I could not change that, because you had to learn something. Before you carry out your final mission for your country you must realize something about yourself and about the Gift."

Jason sat sullenly. "What?" he asked.

"How are your time jumps? Accurate?" Yos asked curiously. Jason swivelled on his chair and stared at the floor.

"No. Not always."

"As it stands, do you think you can complete the mission by yourself?"

"No. Not with my — time-jumping errors," Jason admitted, seeming to melt a little in his chair.

"Why didn't you tell your brother about this morning's task?"

"Dunno. Just felt I had to do it all by myself, I s'pose." Jason shrugged and look up at Yos. Yos was gazing at him sympathetically.

"Anything else?" added Yos quietly.

"Helena. I got Troy to — tell her off for using the Time Twister — because she's a girl. Even though she rescued me anyway. Gee, she's so good at it!"

Yos was grinning, and there were tears in his eyes. When Jason looked up again there were tears in his eyes too.

"Well done, Jason! The mission can now proceed." They embraced warmly.

"But I need help!" protested Jason.

"Exactly! And help has arrived. Come in, Helena."

In the doorway stood a tall, handsome woman dressed in a stylish pair of grass-green overalls. She wore glasses, but Jason immediately saw a similarity to Yos. Helena was with her. Yos and the woman exchanged a look that must have held a thousand words, then she silently departed. Helena came forward. "Howdy, pardner," she said jokingly, and shook Jason by the left hand since his right was still bandaged. Jason grinned sheepishly.

"Together you'll make a formidable team, with Jason on computer and Helena on timing. COMPLOK will never know what hit them. Well, shall we make a start?" suggested Yos enthusiastically.

"Why not?" said Helena looking at Jason.

"Yeah, right! Let's go!" said Jason, his face shining with renewed hope.

"Then may I have your undivided attention, please. Your main task will take place in the PRC room at the University Computing Centre. This is an exact replica of that room. Jason, your task is to load this program into the computer." Yos held up a slim packet that Jason recognized as a floppy disk. "This took years to develop," continued Yos. "If you think of COMPLOK's Master Program as a disease, then this is an innoculation. It resembles the Master Program in every way and behaves the same, but as COMPLOK extends its influence its activities will begin to reveal themselves, as a disease is revealed by its symptoms. Various authorities will then be able to trace these things back to COMPLOK, probably within weeks, and the operation will be undone. But first you must gain access to their program through this." He indicated the palm print security lock. "Jason, do you remember the morning when you first saw this?"

"Yes. It was Tuesday. Gee it seems like ages ago!"

"Yes, it would," said Yos. "What time did the installation technician put his keys down."

"Keys? Let's see . . . that's right! I looked at my watch! It was eight forty-two."

"Exactly?"

"Yes, because it just changed on my digital watch as I looked at it."

"Remember that, Helena. You will be getting the keys. Jason will file his handprint into the print sensor earlier that morning, while the technician is out having a cigarette. Helena will explore through time to discover exactly when he does this. There should be just enough time for Jason to gain entry to the machine and shuffle its memories about with this." Yos held up a small gadget with a tiny screen and buttons and a multicoloured wire with a wide, multi-pin plug on the end. Jason immediately guessed what it would do.

"A hidden file!" he exclaimed. Yos laughed. Once again it seemed as if he found everything to be a huge, private joke.

"Yes, Jason. You're always quick when it comes to computers, aren't you? Well, you've got your work cut out for you this time. For the next four hours I'm going to drill you, step by step, until *you* work like a computer. Time is tight. There will be no room for errors – or hesitation."

"But what about this morning?" queried Helena. "Won't that business with the tape put COMPLOK on their guard?"

"Yes, from Friday on – but we'll be working before then, won't we?"

"Aaah, of course!"

"Good. Let's have a hot drink," said Yos, rising. "Something to sharpen your wits. Then it's time for some real work."

★ ★ ★

Jason lay drowsily in bed, listening to the wind which blustered around the house whipping the rain against his bedroom window with each gust. It was three a.m. and he curled up against the chill of the early morning. Hearing the wind and rain he felt sad that summer was over. In just over a week the second school term would begin — the winter term.

He thought about yesterday and tomorrow, tossing and turning as he tried to get warm and comfortable so he could go back to sleep. Images tumbled through his sleep-befuddled mind: keyboards, screens, codes, sequences, Yos and Helena and the mysterious woman in green. He slipped into a semi-dreamlike state where time was an endless length of computer punched tape, looping and twisting as he ran down it, leaping the holes which got bigger and bigger . . .

He must have finally slept. When he woke to a wet, grey dawn he discovered that he had an extra quilt on his bed but had no idea who had put it there. The telephone rang and he was dimly aware of his father's voice answering it. He looked across at the other bed but Troy wasn't there.

Dragging himself down to the kitchen Jason discovered that both Troy and Helena were already up. They sat in the cosy warmth of the kitchen gazing silently out at the driving rain. Jason didn't particularly like the idea of going out in it but knew he had to. In actual fact, he wasn't feeling very well. His throat felt raw, his head heavy, and he was cold. He was glad when Troy announced that he would go with him – at least as far as he could.

They finished breakfast and stood up to go just as Dave sat down with his coffee. "Hang on," he said to Jason, "that was the COMPLOK Security Chief on the phone earlier. They apparently had a break-in at the Computer Centre last night, and they're clamping down on security while they investigate. So, no computer time this morning, I'm afraid. Actually, I'm quite glad about that really, since I have plans of my own for you this morning."

Jason's heart sank. What was going wrong now?

"Since you're all up, I assume no one wants to sleep in this morning, so I want you all to strip your beds and make them up with clean sheets – the winter flannelette ones. And you can tidy your rooms and the lounge – it's a pig sty in there. Things have been a bit slack recently, kids, haven't they? Now, what else . . . ? Laundry. Troy, are those your dirty clothes in the tub? Dishes, oven, carpets . . . " Dave ticked the chores off on his fingers. "Jason, you can vacuum yours and Troy's room first. Don't forget to empty the vacuum cleaner before you start. Right everyone, let's go! Chop, chop!"

"Aaw, Dad . . ."

"But . . ."

"No buts," said Dave firmly. "Move!"

Chapter ten

"Now what?" said Troy in exasperation.

"Don't panic," replied Jason, dumping the vacuum cleaner on the floor. "I've already got an idea. Anything is possible with this," and he carefully pulled out his time helmet. "What's Dad doing?"

"He's in the kitchen cleaning out the pantry. He'll be occupied for a while." Troy shut the door just to be on the safe side. Suddenly Helena popped into existence in the middle of the room between the two boys. Troy leapt back in fright and sat down with a thud on his bed in the corner. "Don't do that!" he gasped. "How did you get in here? Oh!" He noticed her time helmet.

"Easy!" she laughed. "I just jumped back to last night – three-thirty to be precise – when you two were asleep. Then I just walked in here and time-jumped back to now!"

"You saw us?" Troy asked, fascinated. She nodded. "Did you see yourself?"

Helena was shattered at the idea. "Oh my . . . I never thought! I would've been asleep at that time, too. I didn't think to look, thank goodness! How weird! Seeing yourself." She stood lost in thought.

"Well, it's possible," said Jason. "Hey! Did you put the quilt on my bed?"

"Oh, yeah," she said. "You looked cold. Ha! I only did that a minute ago, my time!"

"Thanks anyway."

"That's okay. Well, let's get going, eh?" suggested Helena with exaggerated confidence.

"Right. When to first, do you reckon?"

"Back to a sunny day!" she exclaimed looking at the driving rain outside.

"Yeah, but we'll need our bikes," said Jason.

"Yeah, right! Hmm – a sunny day when our bikes were here but we weren't . . . "

"Sunday!" Troy cut in. "We were all up at McArthur's Park."

"Good thinking. Sunday, say – midday." Jason turned to Troy. "Sorry you can't come with us."

"No problem," said Troy boldly. He jumped up and clapped Jason on the back then slumped back onto his bed. He drew his knees up under his chin and picked intently at the toe of his track shoe. He felt envious, angry, useless. His voice caught huskily as he added, "Good luck!" He didn't look up.

"Thanks," said Jason gently. He put on his helmet and pulled on his little back pack.

"Follow me, partner," said Helena touching her helmet to his.

★ ★ ★

They opened the garage and went inside. "Seems funny, stealing our own bikes, doesn't it?"

laughed Jason as they wheeled them out. Helena agreed, and they rode off to the University in high spirits.

It didn't take long to time-jump back to 1963 and enter the half-built Computer Centre and soon they were in the PRC room, where they jumped forward to late on Sunday night. They were only one day away from their first task: cracking the palm-print security lock.

Jason laid out the miniature computer on the desk ready for action and Helena let herself out into the machine room. "Time to explore," she said quietly. Her voice quivered slightly.

Jason followed her. "Stand behind this," he suggested. "You'll be in the shadows, but you should be able to see both the technician and the clock clearly."

"Okay," she said, and took up her position behind the Prime Computer tape drives. She took a deep breath and slowly released it. "Right. Tomorrow night from about four a.m. until dawn, preferably later than earlier."

Helena must have made dozens of time jumps but to Jason she just flickered, then turned slowly towards him. He glimpsed a strange, new depth in her eyes. In a peculiar, flat voice she said, "Five twenty-two to five thirty-one."

"You all right?" asked Jason. She didn't reply but looked away.

"Now for the keys," she said a little more normally. She took up the carefully calculated

123

position in the PRC room. Jason sat in the chair as he had been on Tuesday morning.

"Yes, that's it," he said after a moment's study. "The little table should be right in front of you."

"Eight forty-two a.m., Tuesday," she said and jumped. Suddenly the big bunch of keys appeared in her hand. "Bingo!" she exclaimed. "I saw you and him! What a mess! The room that is." She was flushed with excitement. "Wow, my heart's racing. That was scary!"

Jason was nervous now. His moment was close. In his sweaty hands he gripped the gadget Yos had given him. As they touched helmets she caught his eye. "Go for it Jase!" she whispered. "Five twenty-two a.m., Tuesday. Go!"

● ● ●

As they time-jumped forward Jason could feel Helena's exacting time sense pulling them to the precise moment. The room was cluttered as if the technician had just walked out in the midst of something. Heart pounding, Jason quickly began his task. The palm-print device was roughly in place and the power was on, although it hadn't yet been wired into the computer. Swiftly he tried the plastic cards on the key-ring, slipping the edge with the brown magnetic strip along the thin slot. The third card was the one. Clunk. Then the key — there were only two small enough to fit the cover panel lock and the first one did it. Jason pushed the multi-pin plug in and it was ready.

Yos had specially built the miniature computer for this moment, having had plenty of time to study the COMPLOK device. Once it gained access it would rapidly reprogram it so that an extra file would be available for Jason's hand print, the additional memory required being borrowed from the in-built test sequence files. But Yos couldn't learn the password from his research, only the user code. So Jason and Helena waited and waited, while the tiny computer tried every possible six-letter word in the language, then every remaining six-letter combination.

Time ticked on. They became worried. At 5.28 Helena began to pace up and down nervously, glancing across the machine room.

It wasn't the time she was worried about, however. It was some strange quirk of destiny that she struggled against. Finally she realized she would have to do it and stopped her pacing. She looked straight across to the Prime tape drives and saw the shadowy figure that stood there. The figure moved and for a moment was well-lit. It was herself, busy watching the foyer.

Helena waved to attract the other Helena's attention. Their eyes met. It was the strangest moment in Helena's life, to look at herself across that peculiar fold in time. Then she felt a flood of sympathy for that earlier Helena and smiled at her, knowing all too well what she was thinking at that time.

"It's in!" Jason suddenly shouted. Helena turned away quickly. Her brother had touched a button and the small screen was soon ready to receive his handprint. Jason placed his left hand onto the touch-sensitive screen. Ten quick heartbeats later, the screen read 'FILED'. Jason tapped another button and the computer finished its high speed task of deception. 'COMPLETED' it winked.

Within seconds Jason had unplugged his miniature computer and closed up the palm-print device. "Get down!" hissed Helena. "He's coming back!" On the floor Jason fumbled with the keys and his gadget. "Let's go!" she whispered urgently. He hugged his things to his chest and let her jump them away.

● ● ●

"Phew! That was close."

"Yeah."

"What were you worried about at the window?" Jason enquired.

"Huh? Oh . . . nothing. I'll tell you later. Maybe. Hey, wasn't that guy a sweety!" She changed the subject abruptly.

"Who? Gavin? Oh, yeah, he was nice enough, I s'pose. Hey! We did it!" He grasped his sister's hands and danced her around the room. "We did it! We did it!"

"Okay, hold on. Stop it! Hey, don't!" Helena didn't feel in the mood for clowning around. "We haven't finished yet."

"It's no sweat now!" grinned Jason.

"All very well for you! You don't have to make forty or fifty more time-jumps," she said, a slight resentment in her voice.

"Yeah, okay. Sorry." Jason calmed down. "Thursday night, midnight to seven a.m. Any time when the guard does his rounds. Okay?"

"All right, I know."

Although to Jason she didn't even seem to have gone anywhere, Helena looked noticeably tired after completing her second exploration through time. Silently she rummaged in his pack and took out the chocolate bars she had thoughtfully packed. She ate one, then started on another. Finally she spoke.

"Every hour, away for seven minutes," she said, her mouth full, "except at three when he takes eleven minutes."

"Good. We'll take that one," said Jason, grabbing the last chocolate bar for himself.

● ● ●

They made the time jump staying crouched. Jason peered about. "All clear," he said, rising cautiously. Helena slumped to the floor, her back against the wall.

"Watch the time for me," said Jason as he made to move away. "Please," he added, and turned to look at her. Helena nodded and gave him an encouraging smile.

Jason had a lot to remember but it all came back to him the moment he unlocked the palm-reading lock. There were two floppy disk drives but the setup didn't allow him to carry out both processes simultaneously, so first he called up the Master Program.

'MASTER PLAN' BY COMPLOK

** WARNING **
THIS IS A CODE AA SECURITY AREA
INCORRECT PASSWORD
WILL ACTIVATE ALARMS
AT COMPLOK CENTRAL
AND LOCAL SECURITY STATION

PASSWORD PLEASE

Jason was unperturbed. He pressed his left hand against the touch-sensitive palm-reading screen.

PASSWORD ACCEPTED
WELCOME TO 'MASTER PLAN' JASON

He called up the program directory and sped through until he found the vital sections that needed to be changed. He slipped the floppy disk into the Number One drive and instructed 'MASTER PLAN' to accept the correction. Finally he hit the 'enter' key and relaxed with a sigh. It was 3:04 a.m. and he had exactly 43 seconds to relax before doing another three processes which would completely mask the changes of program from anyone without the correct recall codes.

Jason finished these by 3:07 a.m., but carried on with lightning speed to initiate the next task. At 3:11 a.m. the entire 'MASTER PLAN' program was encoded onto the floppy disk that his father had given him on Monday, and the two helmeted children vanished into the night.

● ● ●

It was Sunday night again. The clock on the machine room wall said 11:56 p.m. Since they had arrived eleven minutes ago Jason had experienced twenty-nine minutes, but Helena had been through more than two hours. She was tired, so it was not surprising that she made her first mistake then.

It was nothing serious, she just happened to be a day out in her calculations and time-jumped to Wednesday morning instead of Thursday morning with the keys. It all happened so fast. Surprised, she stepped back, time-jumped again and there in front of her was the cluttered room, the COMPLOK technician and Jason. She tossed the keys carelessly and missed the little trolley, but jumped away quickly as they clattered to the floor.

"Let's go," she mumbled to Jason. "I'm dead tired."

● ● ●

They jumped back to the warmth of Sunday afternoon and rode their bikes home, replacing them carefully in the same places in the garage. They let themselves into the deserted house and headed to their bedrooms. "I'll jump back to now from my own room," said Helena "and get on with tidying it up. See you soon."

"Okay. Hey, Helena!" She turned towards him. "Thanks partner," said Jason softly. She held his eye for a moment and smiled. Jason shuffled nervously. "See you later," he said gruffly. They turned into their separate rooms and put on their time helmets for the last time.

●   ●   ●

Troy hadn't moved a millimetre. "Where's Helena?" he asked.

"In her own room," replied Jason.

"Is it all done?" said Troy with surprise.

"Not quite. There's one more thing – you can do it yourself, if you like," said Jason wearily.

"Yeah, sure – anything!" said Troy eagerly.

Jason eased off his helmet and stretched out on the bed. "Vacuum the floor," he said.

Chapter eleven

"Jason! The helmets have gone!" Helena shook him anxiously.

He had only just dropped off to sleep. His sore throat had worsened and he knew it wouldn't be long before he was really in the grips of a cold. They had decided to wait until the afternoon before reporting back to Yos. After all, time was on their side – or so they believed.

"What? Gone?" He sat up abruptly.

"Mine disappeared while I was in my room, it must have! I just looked around and it was gone. Yours has too, I've already looked." She was on the verge of tears.

"Where could they have gone?" asked Jason.

"They've gone back!" Helena said with conviction. "C'mon, we've got to get to the Time Twister."

They ran through the rain, and arrived puffing and dripping wet. The Time Twister was still there. It lit up as soon as they approached it, and the words on the screen caught their attention.

JASON – HELENA

IT IS ALL OVER
AS IT HAS JUST BEGUN FOR YOU.
THANK YOU BOTH, AND TROY.
IT WAS VERY SPECIAL TO MEET YOU
AND SAD TO SAY GOODBYE.
REST ASSURED THAT YOU WILL
COME TO KNOW US VERY WELL IN THE FUTURE.
PURSUE YOUR STUDIES AND COMPLETE
THE CYCLE FOR YOUR YOUNGER SELVES.
ALL THINGS MUST RETURN
TO THEIR PROPER TIMES,
EXCEPT YOUR MEMORIES.
SO IT MUST BE.

GOODBYE
YOU WILL ALWAYS BE PART OF US.

And before their eyes the Time Twister winked out of existence. There was a loud 'pop' as the air rushed to fill the vacuum of space. In the silence that followed Jason felt Helena's hand gripping his. He didn't look round, as his eyes were full of tears.

The weather seemed to take pity on them as they walked sadly home. It had stopped raining and the sun was promising to break through.

"I wonder what it all meant? 'Complete the cycle' and 'It's all over and just begun'?" Helena pondered.

"'Complete the cycle for your younger selves' it said."

"Yeah . . . 'your younger selves' . . . "

They walked on in silence. "Who was Yos? He looked so familiar," said Jason suddenly.

"She," Helena corrected him.

"No, *he*. Yos was the man!"

"But . . . it was her! The first thing she said to me was 'Just call me Yos'."

"So did he!"

"They were both called Yos? How odd!" remarked Helena.

"Did she say that she was Yos too?"

"Yes! I just told you! She was Yos to me, and he was Yos to you. Yos . . . Yos . . . Y-O-S . . . the initials could stand for something . . . wait on!" Helena's eyes suddenly widened, and she stopped walking. Jason turned to her.

"Your Older Self!" they said simultaneously. Just then the sun broke through and spotlighted the two young people on the cold, autumn street.

"Good grief!" whispered Helena.

"My older self!" exclaimed Jason. "Jeez – my older self!"

Later the rain began again and they had to stay indoors all afternoon. The time seemed to crawl by as is often the case on a cold, wet, miserable afternoon in the middle of the school holidays.

To Jason and Helena the everyday world now seemed like a dream as they drifted aimlessly about the house, lost in their thoughts. Troy knew how they felt and wisely said nothing. Their father, however, kept enthusiastically suggesting activities that they could all do together. "Hey! Let's play Monopoly!" "Troy, what about your slot cars?" "Who wants to help me do some baking?" No one was interested. Finally they agreed to go to the movies, but it turned out to be too late for the two o'clock session and too early for the five o'clock one, so they all just moped about, killing time. They watched some television, they raided the fridge.

Jason's cold grew worse and worse and he hunched beside the heater with a box of tissues, coughing and sniffling.

Dave eventually gave up on trying to amuse his children and settled down to catch up on some reading. After a time, he suddenly put down his book and said, "Helena – did you vacuum your room this morning as I asked you to?"

"Ah . . . well, no."

"Why not?"

"I couldn't find the vacuum cleaner," she replied lamely. "It wasn't in the cupboard."

"Jason – where's the vacuum cleaner?" Dave asked wearily.

"Oh. It's in our room. I forgot to put it back."

Dave MacArthur sighed in exasperation. "Honestly, sometimes I wonder about you kids! God knows what's going to happen to you."

"So do we," mumbled Jason.

"What was that, Jase?"

"So do we . . . wonder what's going to happen, I mean," and he burst into a fit of uncontrollable coughing.

"You won't make it past tomorrow, by the sound of that cough!" joked Dave.

"Oh, yes I will," Jason spluttered. "I can assure you of that!"

ALIENS IN THE FAMILY
Margaret Mahy

0 590 70557 1   £1.50

Bond is in trouble. He is being chased, and his pursuers are powerful and dangerous. When Dora, Lewis and Jake help him, he's grateful, but fears for their safety. Getting Bond to a lonely place beyond the city turns into a far greater adventure than any of the children dream of, but even when lonely, defensive Jake guesses the truth, they are all the more determined to succeed.

THE DANCING METEORITE
Ann Mason

0 590 70541 5   £1.50

Kira Warden is the most talented E-Comm in the system. She can chat to any alien in any language in the system, but science is *not* her strong point. But, when Kira sees a dancing meteorite she knows enough to realize that she has seen the impossible! And a moving meteorite could destroy the whole space station!

Kira *has* to warn them!